What others are saying about *An UnCivil War* — *The Boys Who Were Left Behind*

I'm sure kids will love learning about the Civil War in this way. I did!
— *Barbara McNichol*
  Writer and Editor

Loved it!
— *Sherry Niermann*
  Producer

As a former teacher and Media Specialist, and now as a book seller, I would highly recommend this book to 5th grade teachers in classroom sets or as a read-aloud to use during their Civil War unit. It lends itself to great discussion on the Civil War issues, differences of opinion, and the myriad of emotions that occur during war time and change.
— *Linda Johnson*
  Bookseller, former teacher

The viewpoint used in this book will engage young children in a way most other books about this period don't.
— *Colleen Moore*
  Bookseller

As a lifelong student of the Civil War, I enjoyed the poignancy of this novel. Today's young adults need to grasp the significance of the Civil War as a defining moment in the total history of the United States. Rebecca Cornwell has grasped the essence of our Civil War.
— *Bob Hegarty*
  Civil War Buff

An UnCivil War
The Boys Who Were Left Behind

By Rebecca Clark Cornwell

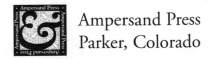

Ampersand Press
Parker, Colorado

An UnCivil War
The Boys Who Were Left Behind

By Rebecca Clark Cornwell

Published by:

Ampersand Press
Post Office Box 3827
Parker, Colorado 80134
USA

AmpersandPress@aol.com
www.BookZone.com/AmpersandPress

This book is a work of fiction. While some of the people, places and events are suggested by historical fact, the story is solely the product of the author's imagination.

ISBN 0-9702449-0-8

Printed in the United States of America

Contents

Acknowledgments

Do it yourself without doing it alone is the motto of the Colorado Independent Publishers Association (CIPA). My name is the one on the cover of this book, but it could easily have a hundred names on it.

Early on, there was Carla Sutton's class who gave me advice about my first draft: Ben, Terese, Harrison, Conor, Amanda, Ben, Trevor, Beth, Mark, Kelly, Rachel, Cameron, Kristina, Christina, Brittney, Kelly, and Christopher.

Bruce Morgan, teacher extraordinaire, made sure I understood my audience.

My cohorts in CIPA helped me every step of the way, willingly and happily encouraging me and teaching me things I never knew I didn't know.

And, of course, there are those people who love me, whose impartiality I don't always trust, but who constantly support my endeavors. My friends and family can always be counted on to give me a kick in the seat or a pat on the back, whichever I might need.

But I especially want to thank the gang I live with
— my very accommodating and patient husband, Wes, who is SuperComputerMan to my TechnoGeek, a happy yin and yang agreement which we both enjoy;
— my daughter, Jessica, who would rather read fantasy but who reads my work anyway;
— my son, Jeffrey, who thinks having a writer for a mother is very cool;
— and maybe most importantly, my son, Adam, for throwing this gauntlet in front of me and forcing me to pick it up.

All of these wonderful people have my gratitude.

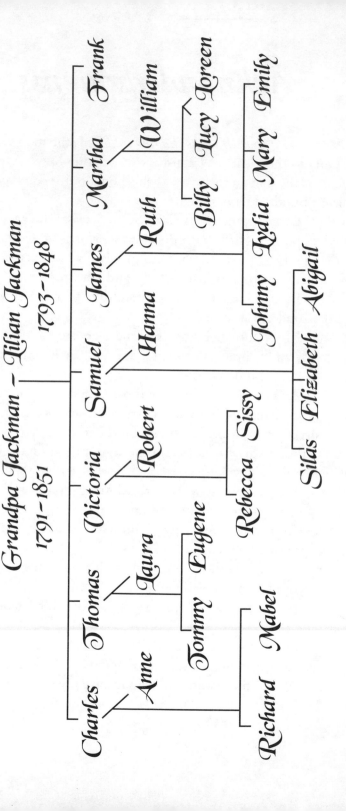

CHAPTER 1

Spring Comes to Virginia, 1860

Winter was finally showing signs of melting into spring, that year of 1860. Industrial cities like New York and Boston were beginning to brighten from their grimy, muddy winter lives. The buds on the trees were opening and early wildflowers were poking through the ground, creating a multi-colored carpet. Bear, deer, skunks and the other animals were shaking off their long winter's sleep.

Rivers were trickling where they had been dry, and rushing where they had been just a trickle. The snow was melting and the grass was turning green.

The state of Virginia was particularly lovely this spring. It was so lovely, in fact, it was hard to imagine the terrible ordeal that would change everything by the time spring rolled around next year.

On the east coast of Virginia, dogwood were blooming and people whistled happily as they went about their business. Near the Ohio River on the western boundary of Virginia, wild strawberries were growing and farm children had thoughts of visiting the swimming hole. Mothers, however, always seem to have different ideas than their kids. "You'll catch your death swimming in that spring run-off! Don't you know that water is melted snow?! And put your shoes back on!" they say, as if part of a chorus.

There weren't many large towns in western Virginia in 1860; in fact, there weren't many towns at all. Mostly the area was dotted with farms, some quite large, with almost 100 acres. Ranchers ran cattle on their spreads, while some farmers had large tobacco crops.

Most of the farms, though, were modest subsistence farms, growing what the family needed to survive plus a little extra to sell to neighbors or to barter with the local tradesmen. If a subsistence farmer needed new shoes for his horse, for example, he would pay the blacksmith with these excess crops. The blacksmith, in turn, needed food for his family since he was busy running the blacksmith shop and didn't have time for tending crops. Everyone was happy with the arrangement and understood their survival depended on each other.

All the large farms and some of the smaller ones had entered the age of mechanization by 1860. A man named John Deere had invented and perfected the steel plow about thirty years earlier. This great technological invention was light enough for a single person to guide it and it cut perfect furrows every time. The more prosperous farmers also had steel-toothed horsedrawn reapers which could do as much work at harvesting time as five men with scythes.

If it was possible to fly over the area, the landscape would have looked like an elaborate patchwork quilt. Flat green fields, chocolate colored fields waiting for a crop, stands of tall trees, patches of snow scattered around — and there were towns, of course, here and there. Some can barely be called towns at all, so small and remote they're only on the map two days a week!

Some towns you might have heard of since they're

pretty big and busy like Winchester and Staunton — both having nearly 4,000 people living there. There was also Parkersburg and Harper's Ferry with populations of about 2,500 people. But most towns were much smaller.

Hadley was a town like that. There was not much to it; just one dirt road running the length of it to serve the farms and families in the area surrounding it.

On that dirt road was Hawkin's General Store with its wooden steps, squeaky screen door constantly slammed shut and shelves lined floor-to-ceiling with everything needed to run a household and a farm. If Abel Hawkins didn't have it in his store, people just didn't need it.

Next to Hawkins' store was the blacksmith shop. The only blacksmith in Hadley was Hiram Smithson, but if you asked anyone, they'd say his name was Smithy. Most folks probably didn't even know he had a Christian name, although if they thought about it, they'd guess his momma and poppa called him something other than "Smithy." They might also wonder if he became a blacksmith just so his name and his job were the same.

But no one ever thought about it.

Abel Hawkins and Smithy mostly got along well enough. But occasionally, when the weather was particularly hot, tempers verged on flaring up over the most trivial problem. Abel was known to storm out of his store and march down the wooden stairs over to the smithy like a banty-legged rooster locked out of the hen house.

"You good-for-nothin' blacksmith! You are driving me and my customers out of my shop. I haven't had one danged customer all day and it's because you're heatin' up this place like my granny's stove top. And everyone *knows* she burned anything she cooked, bless her soul!"

Then the blacksmith would stomp out of his shop, sweat streaming off his face and neck. He'd pull his heavy leather gloves off as he walked and begin punctuating the air with them, making his point. "No sirree, Abel Hawkins! You can't blame the weather on me this time! Did you ever consider you have no customers because it's too darned hot to come to town? And how do you expect me to work without my fire goin'?"

Before the argument got much past this stage, someone would saunter over to Hawkins' store and say, "Hey, Abel, you got any of them licorice whips I like so much?"

The townsfolk had heard this argument so many times over the years, they began to think it was just a show Abel and Smithy put on periodically. Maybe it was their way of beating the heat on a summer day.

But Hadley was a place where people watched out for one another and no one would have let the two men get into a true fight. Especially about the weather — there were enough *real* things to argue about. People had their disagreements in Hadley but, like every farming community, everyone pulled together whenever they needed to, usually on short notice.

Across from the blacksmith shop under some huge old chestnut trees stood the church. Everyone called it "the meetin' house," though. It was the hub of social life of the town. Sunday mornings and Wednesday evenings, it was used for worship.

Many in the town would like it to house a school during the week, but there weren't enough children in the area who could come into town on a regular basis. So many of them were needed to work at home that it's wishful thinking they could have a full-time school *with* an actual trained teacher. Most of the children, if they got any education at all, would get it from their mothers, but only when it's convenient.

Throughout the week, the church was used for town business, but Saturday afternoons and evenings would find it full of people laughing and carrying on in various social situations. Sometimes there might be a dance or a town picnic. Or an ice cream social. And once, when they were trying to raise money to buy a bell for the steeple, the towns-people tried to have a box social. That's when the women packed a secret picnic lunch and the men bid money for it. Afterward, all the money would be donated to the "Bell Fund." However, it didn't quite work out the way they planned because no one had any money to spare. So the "bids" included barter items like a chicken or two gallons of milk or a bushel of corn. They didn't make any money for their bell, but everyone had lots of fun.

So, the pretty white church across from the smithy had a steeple, but no bell. Pastor Schum just told everyone, "When the Good Lord wants us to have a bell, He'll let us know."

Next to the church, across from Abel Hawkins' store was the train stop. It couldn't even be considered a train "station" because there wasn't even a building there. It was literally just a stop — just a dusty place near the road. The train tracks ran behind the church and the train stop.

Trains didn't come through Hadley very often and they stopped even less. Not many people wanted to visit or leave Hadley. If someone wanted to get on the train and go away from town, they'd have to talk to Abel Hawkins who would rummage through his "ticket drawer" to find a ticket for you. He knew he didn't have any valid tickets to any-where, but it made him feel important to rummage around and look for one. In the end, he always had to look on his well-worn chart for the price to wherever his customer wanted to go, then find a scrap of paper to write it down. The traveler had to go to the stop and raise the red flag to signal the conductor to stop, then pay for his ticket on the train.

No one ever wondered why Abel Hawkins had to be involved in the transaction. They had always done it that way.

Things change slowly in small towns in 1860.

So that was the entire town of Hadley. A store and a blacksmith across from a church and the train stop. It was all anyone needed around there.

Chapter 2

Business Decisions

Before he died, Grandpa Jackman — which is what everyone in Hadley called him, whether they were related to him or not — ran sheep on the land covering what is now two different farms owned by two of his grown sons, James and Samuel.

They both helped with the sheep, but when Grandpa died in 1851, nine years earlier, he left half the land to James and half to Sam.

Sam assumed they would continue on as before, but James had other ideas.

James had gone to Sam's one day soon after Grandpa's affairs had been settled. He was very excited. "Sam! Where are you! Come take a look at this!" yelled James as he got close to Sam's farmhouse.

Sam came outside with a half-eaten biscuit in his hand. Leaning against the porch railing, he laughed. "You look like you just won the blue ribbon at the county fair, little brother! What in the world has you so worked up?"

James handed Sam an envelope full of papers. As Sam took them out and began to unfold them, James couldn't wait and began talking excitedly. James was talking fast and Sam was trying to read so he was only able to hear bits and pieces of what his brother was saying.

"This here's our future, Sam. Look at how pretty those trees are . . . they're apple trees . . . lots of different kinds . . . plant them now . . . my half of the farm . . . won't have any apples for ten years or so . . . I'll need your help . . . oooh, that's a pretty little orchard!"

"Hold on, hold on!" Sam interrupted him. "You mean to tell me you don't want to raise sheep anymore? You want to experiment with apple trees that you don't know anything about? We know everything there is to know about sheep but you want to throw that all away?"

The angry look on Sam's face sucked the excitement right out of James. He looked as if he'd been slapped.

Sam said in a low, menacing voice, "If you think I'm going to give up everything I've worked so hard for just so you can play with some . . . some . . . trees that won't make us any money . . . well, it's just not going to happen."

Sam looked disgustedly at the biscuit still in his hand and threw it into the yard, clomped up the stairs and slammed the door behind him. James folded all the papers about the apple trees and stuffed them back into the envelope they came in.

Weeks went by with the two brothers not speaking to one another, yet continuing to take care of the sheep together. Sam really wasn't angry any longer that James wanted an orchard, but because of James' sullenness, was a little afraid to talk to him. Sam just assumed James would come around to his way of thinking.

However, he didn't think it would take this long! Usually when they had any disagreement it would only last a day or two — not several weeks. Sam was beginning to worry about it, but had no idea what to do. This was a sheep ranch, not an apple orchard.

Sheep are what we know. Sheep are profitable, thought Sam. And James knows that.

One day when they both were mending the fence, Sam glanced over and watched James work. The look on James' face broke Sam's heart. It was obvious James was unhappy.

Sam went back to his own work, but now his brain was engaged, clicking away, trying to work out a solution to this problem.

Finally, he called over to his brother, saying "James, come here. We need to talk."

James slowly took off his work gloves and held them in his hand as he ambled over to where Sam stood.

"James, I've been thinking," Sam began.

James rolled his eyes, expecting Sam to begin a lecture on how his mind wasn't on his work, he was slackin' off, not doing his share . . .

Imagine his surprise when he heard Sam say, "I think we can make an orchard work for both of us."

James' eyes got as big as saucers. He was speechless. "I . . . I . . . think we can, too!" he managed to squeak out.

Sam laughed and put an arm around his brother's shoulder. "I'm thinkin' we can make a deal. What if you keep helpin' me with these sheep while I help you plant some of those silly apple trees. We'll have to sell some of the sheep to buy the trees, but that's okay since we won't have as much land to run them on anyway."

"I'll figure out what I owe you and whenever the orchard begins to produce, I'll start paying you back," James looked at Sam gratefully.

"It shouldn't be too much since you'll still be helping me with the sheep." Both men were getting excited about their new opportunity.

Suddenly James asked, "But what changed your mind?"

Sam tried to explain his feelings when he saw the hurt in James' eyes earlier, but couldn't find the right words. Instead he said simply, "It just seems like a good business decision."

That was a lie, of course, because that day in his yard when he was eating his biscuit, he never even let James explain how they could make an orchard work.

So James began to talk about how they had the opportunity, as brothers with adjoining land, to produce two varied products, which would be the diversification necessary to survive in the world of farming and ranching.

"Diversifi - what?!" Sam asked.

"Diversification. It's how you don't tie yourself down to only one crop. What if the sheep all died? We'd have nothing. Or what if more people begin to raise sheep. Then the prices for our wool will fall and we'd make a lot less profit. But if we have sheep **and** an orchard, then the odds of success are with us," James explained.

Sam began to catch on. "So, if we start now to plant the orchard — and really do it right — then in ten years we'll have a great orchard as well as great sheep."

"Right! We're just lucky we have so much land and can help each other until the orchard produces," said James.

So after weeks of silence between them, now they were both talking at once, making plans for "their" orchard.

And that's how they came to work together to have two different farms. It was a situation they both liked — which is not to say it was easy.

Mostly, they agreed on the important aspects of their business and early on had accepted one main rule: Whatever decisions made had to be fair to both families.

On occasion, however, they had differences of opinion.

Probably the worst moment came when Sam wanted to buy more sheep but James didn't think they had enough money. Some hurtful things were said by both men and they almost used their fists, but they were brothers, after all. When they calmed down, they compromised and joked about it . . . after some time passed, that is.

Sam was less than a year older than James, but never let him forget it. Even though they were both adults — and had been for some time — Sam would still tell James, "You have to respect your elders and that includes getting me another cup of coffee, Youngster!" Sometimes when James got tired of catering to his brother's wishes, he would "accidentally" put salt in Sam's coffee instead of sugar. That usually gave Sam the hint and he put no more demands on James. They loved each other fiercely in spite of their different personalities.

And they were determined to make their businesses work — Sam concentrating on the sheep and James concentrating on the orchard.

CHAPTER 3

James Jackman's Family

From working in their fields every day, the Jackmans were muscular and tanned. From God, they've received the gift of good looks — James in particular. He had dark brown hair that curled just right around his head and neck. He had his wife trim it, though, when it escaped into the collar of his shirt and tickled him.

Sometimes it would get bored and, instead, curl into an ear to aggravate him. One time, in fact, he was repairing a ladder and just as he was striking with the hammer, his hair tickled his ear. He flinched and ended up with a black and blue thumbnail. He stomped into the house muttering things his children shouldn't hear, grabbed the offending lock of hair and cut it off with his wife's good sewing scissors. At the time, no one dared laugh at his lop-sided haircut, but his good humor came back at about the same time his thumb's swelling went down.

It's possible that the Jackman's attractiveness stems from their happy nature and fun sense of humor. With his four brothers and two sisters, James grew up in a happy house full of mostly good-natured teasing and jokes, which was perfectly acceptable to their parents as long as it didn't get in the way of the work to be done.

Now that the Jackmans have families of their own, they've continued the tradition. In spite of the difficulties each of them face, their households were rarely somber. It was a lesson they learned from Grandpa who constantly said things like "when God gives you lemons, make lemonade" and "a good laugh is sunshine in a house."

James had his own particular silly talent, which he used to amuse his children on a regular basis. He could imitate the sound of any bird or animal and often creates ridiculous faces and mannerisms to go along with them. His "bear getting stung by bees" would get almost as many requests as his "porcupine in love."

James had been working hard to establish the apple orchard since 1851 when it all started. He was lucky, though; he saw indications that he'd be able to pick apples soon — some orchards don't produce for twelve years!

James lived there with his wife, Ruth, and his four children.

He was leaning on a fence post near the barn taking a break from chopping wood. As he looked around his farm, he smiled. Everything he loved was within sight.

He watched his beautiful wife, Ruth, hanging the wash on the clothes line to dry. He saw her take something from the basket. Snap it hard. Pin it to the line with exactly six clothespins — no more, no less. Pick up another wet something. Snap it. Pin it. Ruth was indeed a creature of habit.

She always wore her thick auburn hair coiled in a braid around the back of her head. James loved to watch her brush and braid her hair. He marvelled at how she could, without even looking, get it all into a perfect braid then pin it up using only four hair pins. One time he joked that her braid must weigh thirty pounds and, if she wanted him to, he could fetch a fence post to help brace it.

Ruth also wore the same clothes every day — a long-sleeved cotton print dress buttoned up to her chin with an apron covering her skirt. She had several dresses and several aprons, but they were all so similar, someone would have to look closely to tell one from the other.

Ruth turned and saw James smiling at her. She stopped her routine long enough to give him a quick wave. James waved back, thinking she looked exactly the same as the day fourteen years before when they married. It seemed like yesterday, yet they had four children now!

Johnny, the oldest, was keeping his younger sisters busy, at Ruth's request, so she could get some of her chores finished.

James smiled at the memory of the conversation at breakfast this morning. Ruth had asked Johnny, "What are your plans today, son?" Everyone knew that meant she had plans for him already. Unless he wanted to be disappointed, his plans should coincide with what his mother wanted!

"Uh . . . uh . . . I was going fishin' . . . " Johnny saw his mother raise her eyebrows and glance sideways at him. "I mean . . . I was . . . uh . . . going to help you do something?"

"What a clever boy you are," joked Ruth.

James felt proud of his son. It's never easy getting everything done on a farm, but they could count on Johnny . . . even when he'd rather go fishing.

In 1860, Johnny was twelve. Not only was he the oldest, he was also the only boy in the family. His parents depended on him to do his share of chores. But he didn't mind hard work. He was getting tall and his muscles were beginning to develop from all his hard work. He had a shock of bright carrot colored hair that he hated. Everyone teased him about it. "Hey, I saw you coming a mile away!" "Quick! Put on a hat! You're hurting my eyes!" He's heard all the jokes — no one said anything original anymore. Mostly the teasing was all in fun, but he still got tired of it.

As much as Johnny hated his red hair, his younger sister, Lydia, loved hers. The eight-year-old loved nothing better than being the center of attention. According to Johnny, though, she was a pest. She really was just a little kid — and a girl at that! — but still expected to go everywhere Johnny went. Mostly, he would just tell Lydia she couldn't go with him and she'd pout a bit, then get over it. But other times she really made a fuss. Sometimes their mother got tired of hearing Lydia whine about going fishing with Johnny so she would take Johnny aside, saying, "Please take her with you so I can get a moment's peace. I'll make it up to you with an extra big slice of apple pie at dinner tonight." Since his mother's apple pie was the most delicious thing in the world, he would do it. But he still thought Lydia was a pest.

Johnny thought six-year-old Mary, on the other hand, was just the right age. She was old enough to play games with if he felt like it, but not so old that her feelings got hurt if he wanted to go somewhere with his friends or just be by himself. If he was in a particularly good mood, Johnny would even offer to have a tea party with Mary and her dolls, just because she was such a good sport — as long as none of his friends could see him, that is.

Johnny, Lydia and Mary loved playing hide-and-seek. The girls only wanted to hide, never to seek, so Johnny played that part with gusto. It was never difficult to find them because they were so noisy about hiding.

Lydia and Mary had two ways to hide. They'd hold hands and run off to hide together, giggling and whispering about the best place. Or they'd go every time to the exact same places where they hid in the last round.

It wasn't a big challenge to win, but Johnny always pretended he couldn't find them. Over the years, that had become one of the unofficial rules of the game.

"Where ARE those girls?" he'd say, after counting to

twenty with his eyes closed. He'd look in the unlikeliest of places, which made the girls giggle even more.

"Oh, I bet they're in this milk can. No, not there. Hmmm, maybe they crawled in that mouse hole. No, not there either."

Soon he'd have wandered around and ended up behind them. The girls seemed to believe that if they kept their eyes shut, he couldn't see them. But when they realized he was closing in on them, they'd scramble up, still giggling, and run to the sycamore tree in the middle of the yard. It served as "home free."

Johnny always let them get there before he did.

Finally, seeing his mother was almost finished with the laundry, he said, "I'll play one more round of hide-and-seek with you, but then I'm going fishing."

He glanced at his mother and got the nod of approval from her. She smiled at Johnny and he winked at her, walking over to his youngest sister.

The baby, Emily, just turned two and looked like Mary, although the blond curls of Mary's infancy were becoming more red every day. Em was adorable with her curly blond hair and big blue eyes, but as far as Johnny was concerned, she had a ways to go before she'd be much fun. Much of the time, she didn't smell very pleasant. Now was one of those times.

"Dang it," he thought to himself. He had planned to play with Em for a couple of minutes to earn some extra points with his mother. Sometimes when he did something unexpectedly helpful, his mother rewarded him with a special treat from the kitchen. Now he had to change a diaper, not at all what he had planned. Little did he know, because he did what needed to be done without a complaint, his mother was already planning to make his favorite dinner.

Yes, James felt proud of his delightful family and beautiful orchard. His life was turning out just the way he had planned it.

CHAPTER 4

Samuel Jackman's Family

Two miles beyond James' farmhouse was where James Jackman's older brother Samuel and his family lived.

Sam and James looked alike — tanned, muscular, blue eyes, dark hair — but instead of curly hair, Sam's was straight. Sam's eyes would crinkle merrily around the corners when he smiled, which he did constantly. With each passing year, the lines get chiseled even more deeply. His wife, Hanna, teased him that when he'd reach 70, he'd just be one big "laugh line." Sam responded by flashing her a smile.

Sam could make the entire family smile simply by reaching for his fiddle, which he kept in a case beside his favorite rocking chair. He said he knows every tune written "and then some" so he could entertain them all night long. When he saw the children get sleepy (or when he wants them to get sleepy), he'd slow down the tempo, send them to bed and they drift off to the melancholy sounds of "Red River Valley" or "Greensleeves." Sometimes he sent them off with a sad, slow lullaby that's not really sad. They'd be just falling asleep when they'd realize he was playing "Happy Birthday" or a dance tune played in half time or in a minor key.

Sam and Hanna had three children. Hanna had dark hair like her husband, but brown eyes instead of blue, and pale porcelain skin — not tanned and lined like Sam's. In fact, Hanna's skin was so fair, she freckled very easily . . . and hated it. She did everything she could think of to keep from freckling. Once, she even bought some thick, smelly green goop in a jar from Abel Hawkins who told her, "This will take care of any . . . er . . . imperfections on your skin." Abel didn't tell her that he, and most men, found her freckles charming.

The goop didn't change anything so her only defense against the sun was to wear a bonnet anytime she stepped out of her house — even just to get a bucket of water from the well! The end of every summer would find her lamenting the fact she has more freckles than last year. Sam teased her about counting them each year for comparison and told her she looked just as beautiful to him. Hanna knew she was being vain and told herself freckles don't really matter . . . but she kept her bonnet handy nonetheless.

Silas, like his cousin Johnny, was twelve and the oldest in his family as well as the only boy. He had straight dark hair that fell into his face when he was working hard.

Silas hated his name. His mother tried to comfort him by telling him he was named after his great grandfather. His father tried to comfort him, too, by joking that all the Jackmans named their firstborn sons with the first letter of their fathers' names, but they couldn't use the same name because it was too confusing. That's why James had 'Johnny' and why Sam had an 'S' name for his son.

A million times he heard his father tell him, "Besides, the only other 'S' name we could come up with was 'Susan' so you should probably thank your lucky stars!" and a million times it made him laugh. Sometimes, though, when he was particularly cranky, he wouldn't let his parents see him smile.

He never realized, though, that they *always* knew he smiled!

Silas was a bit jealous of Johnny because he wasn't growing quite as quickly as his red-headed cousin. Because they were so close in age, their play took the form of rivalry and competition more often than not. However, it seemed more and more that Johnny was able to wrestle him into a head lock without much effort.

Silas was strong, but not as tall as he'd like to be. Every night before hopping into bed, he'd kneel down, fold his hands and pray, "God, please bless Mama and Papa and the girls and all the other Jackmans in the world. I'm also hopin' you're fixin' to make me taller one of these days. I know you're pretty busy, but any day now would be fine with me. Thank you. Oh, and bless all the animals too." On days when he felt particularly jealous of his cousin Johnny, he added, "And thank you for not giving me that crazy orange hair."

That always made him feel better.

Elizabeth was five and Silas adored her. With her dark hair and dark eyes, she looked just like a miniature version of their mother. A very calm child, she liked to talk to Silas as he did his chores. He was amazed at some of the thoughts in her clever little head. He enjoyed their conversations most of the time, but sometimes she wore him out with her questions and her opinions.

Three-year-old Abigail was quite a different story, however. Though she also had straight dark hair and big dark eyes, she was as rowdy and rambunctious as her sister was calm. Mama joked that Abigail tried to take care of Elizabeth's share of the noise as well as her own. Many times Silas was asked to help with his youngest sister. "Silas, go outside and let Abbey chase you. If we wear her out, maybe she'll take a nap today." If Silas complained, his mother threatened to put Abbey in *his* room to play. The thought of his sister let loose in his room always brought him around! "No, Mama! That's okay, I'd *love* to play with her!"

CHAPTER 5

Uncle Cowboy

"Hey ya'll gather 'round here! We got a letter from Frank!" Sam yelled. He and James had gone to town together for supplies. Whenever they needed supplies, he would bring Hanna and the children to visit with James' family, then they'd all have dinner together.

At the mention of a rare letter, everyone dropped what they were doing and ran to the men. The excitement in their voices caused even the little ones, Abigail and Emily, to come on the run — and neither one of them even knew what a letter was! It was probably safe to say that receiving a letter was rare enough that it hadn't ever happened in two-year old Emily's life.

Distance meant a lot in 1860 and families rarely saw each other if they moved away. Those who could write tried to keep up with each other by letter. Members of the Jackman family were lucky, though. They had been taught to read and write by their mother.

These skills of reading and writing, although none of

them would realize it for several months, would become the most important thing in their lives. And the delivery of rare pieces of mail to Hadley would become less rare.

It was a long process getting a piece of mail to and from a town in those days. Hadley's trains ran on a more-or-less regular basis. Mail was delivered whenever the train stopped there.

In the 1860s, the people who received the mail had to pay for it instead of those who sent a letter. For that reason, there were secret codes people had worked out where they would write something on the outside of the letter. The recipient, the person the letter was written to, would read the outside of the letter, get the information the person was sending, then hand the letter back to the postmaster saying they didn't want the letter. In a time when not much money was available to people, they saved many coins by not paying for letters.

It was much more difficult to get mail to and from Uncle Frank, however, because he rarely lived near a town, and often the nearest town had no regular train service.

Frank was Sam's and James' youngest brother. He had the most interesting job, according to the children of the family. He was a cowhand in Texas. The life of a farmer never appealed to Frank as it did to Sam and James.

Frank spent much of his time either on a cattle drive moving cattle from one place to another, or out with the cattle on the large ranch in east Texas where he worked. One thing was for certain, though, everyone looked forward to hearing about Frank's escapades. Johnny and Silas were especially interested in their Uncle Frank's life. It all seemed so glamorous and fun. In reality, it was neither. He had a difficult job and lifestyle being on the trail.

"Read it, read it, read it!" chanted the children when everyone had gathered around the kitchen table. "Hold your horses, I'm trying to open it!" said Sam, carefully sliding his finger under the flap so he wouldn't tear the precious paper inside. "Okay, here goes!"

Dear Family,

I trust this letter finds you happy and healthy and busy with your farms. I was just thinking the other day that it's about time for those apple trees to start producing, isn't it? I haven't had a good apple in longer than I can remember!

I am as well as can be expected out here in hot, dusty Texas. Yes, I said "hot." Even though you're barely feeling the effects of spring, it's already hot here! We hardly get any winter.

I thought I'd better sit down and let you know what I've been up to and what's coming up for me. I don't want you to forget about poor old Frank!

There are millions of long-horned cattle all over Texas. The market for cattle is in the North and East part of the country. Unfortunately, there's no railroad linking Texas with those parts of the country so in a few weeks I'll be on a huge cattle drive to the nearest railroad. Then we leave the cattle to be taken by rail to Kansas City or Chicago to the meat-packing plants.

Actually, I don't mean to brag, but your little brother got promoted to Trail Boss for this trip. I'll be in charge! How about that?

Before we go, me and the boys have to round up, then brand the cattle. And when I say "boys," I mean boys! I'm just but 31 this year and they call me an old-timer. Most cowhands here are in their late teens or early 20s, and have to be strong and fearless. Only the cooks are older than me!

Silas interrupted, "Aw gee, I want Uncle Frank to keep bein' a cowboy."

Hanna scolded her son. "Shame on you. Your Uncle Frank earned his position of authority by many years of hard work, many gallons of sweat and blisters too many to count, so I don't want you talking so selfish about him doin' better for himself." To her husband she said, "Go ahead, Sam."

Sam scanned ahead in the letter. "Well, don't worry. It sounds like he's doin' the same job as the cowhands. I guess he's just in charge of makin' decisions now."

It will take about three months to get the cattle from here to Kansas. We'll be in the saddle 18 hours every day, with no days off.

I don't think you've ever seen what I wear to work, have you? Everything we wear has to be practical. Our boots have pointed toes to slip easily into our stirrups, thin soles to get a good feel of the stirrups, and high heels to grip the stirrup firmly. We wear chaps to protect our legs when we go through thick brush. We wear wide-brimmed hats to shield us from branches, sun and rain. Our bandanas have many uses, limited only by our imagination and needs! A bandana protects our necks from sunburn, keeps the dust out of our mouth and nose, and keeps our ears warm. I've even seen Cook strain coffee through his! I didn't drink any coffee that day, but I came to find out he did it every day so I figured, well, it hasn't killed me yet so I'm back to drinking Cook's coffee again.

Ruth and Hanna exchanged glances. Ruth said, "I hope he gets to town every once in a while to get better coffee!"

We've had lots of times on trail rides when we've gotten kicked by horses, trampled in stampedes and practically drowned crossing rivers, so I guess coffee drinking isn't my biggest worry.

When you wrote last, the boys wanted to know about the Indians out here, but you needn't worry about that. There are many Indians here, but very few make any trouble for us. Mr. Owens, the rancher I work for, treats every man with respect and makes sure we do, too. They are people just like us, trying to feed their families and live a good life. In fact, I'd say more cowboys are killed by lightning than by Indians.

I will tell you what I __am__ afraid of, boys. Cattle rustlers. I don't know if you've heard of them, but they are lawless and lazy

*men who would rather steal someone else's cattle than sweat a
little raising their own. There isn't much law out here and what
little there is, these men don't care about.*

*Gunfights are pretty common in the frontier towns along
the trail so my boys and I stay away from towns as much as
possible. These thieves come in the dead of night where we've
camped so we post sentries to scare them away if they mess with
our cattle. If they don't go away, Mr. Owens gave us orders to
shoot to kill, hopefully before they shoot us. We've had run-ins
with rustlers, but so far, we've never had any shootin' to do. And I
hope we never do. None of us relish the idea of getting killed or
killing another man, even if he is stealing our cattle.*

*The bunkhouse is quiet now and I've got an early day
tomorrow. Just thought I'd let you know how I'm getting on. I also
wanted to tell you I'll do my best to get out your way for Christmas.
Everything around here should be done by then so I can talk to Mr.
Owens about letting me go for a while. It will be great if everyone
can be together this year for the holidays. We haven't done that since
we were little kids! I'm looking forward to seeing all of you Hadley-
ites as well as Charles, Thomas and the girls.*

Charles and Thomas are two more Jackman brothers
and "the girls" are their two sisters, Victoria and Martha.
They've been planning for a year already to get everyone to
Hadley for Christmas. With Charles in Baltimore, Thomas in
Philadelphia, Victoria in South Carolina and Martha in
Atlanta, it's quite an adventure in planning.

*Take good care of the little ones and say a prayer for me
once in a while.*
Love,
Frank

Johnny and Silas thought Frank had the best job
imaginable, but neither would admit he'd ever want to do it
himself.

CHAPTER 6

Tree Planting

The sky was bright blue, but the wind howled across the orchard. James and Johnny were planting their new apple trees this blustery March day in 1860. Johnny's red hair was being blown into an even messier cap of curls than he normally wore. Even though Johnny was tall and strong, he struggled against the wind.

"Next year, let's not plant until the winds die down!" shouted James to his son.

Johnny agreed, "I'll hold you to it!"

The seedlings arrived packed in moss and wrapped in burlap. It was Johnny's job to unwrap them, snip off the unhealthy roots and lay them near the holes his father had dug.

When he was done unwrapping and inspecting them all, he called out to his father, "Pa, they're ready!" His father leaned on his shovel. He surveyed the job Johnny had done. "I reckon you can handle the trimming, too," he shouted.

Johnny couldn't believe what he heard. "You mean it?" he asked excitedly.

"Sure! I think you're old enough to do a good job. You've seen it done practically every year since you could walk!" James replied.

Every year they plant some new trees to replace dead or diseased ones. It also ensures the continuity of the orchard.

Suddenly, Johnny got a stricken look on his face. "Will you stay and watch to make sure I do it right?" Johnny did not trust himself nearly as much as his father seemed to. After all, it takes at least ten years of constant care for an apple tree to produce any apples. He didn't want to be responsible for the entire crop of new apple trees.

Johnny's father walked over to him and slung an arm around his shoulder. "Son, I would never ask you to do something I didn't think you were ready to do. But, if *you* don't think you're ready . . ."

"Yeah, I can do it," Johnny said, brightening. Silently he added, "If you think I can then I will."

The trimming wasn't exactly difficult, but it was the outward manifestation of a tree-trimmer's skills. It showed exactly how he did the job. No one could see if he dug a crooked hole or left a little moss on the roots. But *everyone* knew if he did a bad trim job! It would be right there for all to see — if it wasn't right, the tree would be crooked and look funny. And it might even make the tree unhealthy.

Johnny needed to trim the branches to make them proportional to the size of the roots. He picked up the clippers in his right hand and the first seedling in his left. He glanced sideways at his father to make sure James was watching. He knew his father wouldn't let him make a mistake — they've worked too hard for nine long years to make this orchard a reality.

Johnny lifted the small tree to make it level with his eyes. He studied it while turning it around and around. Snip, snip, turn, and one more snip.

"There!" Johnny lifted it up and turned it around for

his father to inspect.

His father studied it, reached for it and studied it some more.

"Hmmm," he murmured.

Johnny began to get nervous, but knew enough to keep quiet while his father was thinking. Just as his palms and forehead began to sweat, he saw his father look at him with a twinkle in his eye and a broad smile on his lips.

"Got ya, didn't I? Made you sweat?" When Johnny nodded, his father said, "Sorry, but you looked so serious, I just couldn't resist! This tree is perfect. You have a good eye for this, son. Maybe I'll just let you do all the work and I'll retire this year."

"Oh, Pa," Johnny tried to look annoyed with his father's joke, but he couldn't. He was so happy to have earned his father's praise.

"But don't look so cocky; there's still a lot of work to do this year. In a couple weeks, we'll need to spread fertilizer. And it looks like the dandelions are getting ready to come up. That means Worthy McKay will be bringing the beehives over here one of these days."

Johnny gave a shudder when he heard that name. If the image of the old man was a knife, it would have pierced Johnny's heart right then and there. In his mind, he saw scary old Worthy wearing his patched and faded overalls, his skin like an old piece of leather, always scowling. Johnny tried to shake the picture from his brain. He hadn't thought about Worthy McKay in a long time. He didn't think his Pa knew about the trouble he and some of his friends had with the old beekeeper the previous year, but it still scared Johnny when he thought about their close call.

Johnny remembered the Saturday last summer when he, his cousin Silas and two of their friends, Toad and Rooster, were down at the pond doing what boys do best — playing, fishing and thinking about food!

Toad and Rooster were brothers. Rooster was a little older than Johnny, Toad a little younger. It occurred to Johnny that these boys, friends of his for years, had very strange names. He'd known them for so long, he couldn't even remember their real names. Surely their mother didn't call them "Toad" and "Rooster!"

His smile turned to a frown when he remembered those fateful words spoken by Rooster — "Let's go get some honey!" Johnny could still picture Silas' face when they looked at each other. They both knew exactly what Rooster meant. He wanted to steal honeycombs from Worthy McKay's honey house.

Both of the Jackman cousins knew how wrong this was, but neither wanted to look like they were scared in front of Rooster and Toad. They both tried to get out of it.

Silas said, "Nah, I want to catch more fish. I told my Ma I'd bring home dinner tonight."

Johnny said, "Yeah, me too."

"You did not. You're just a couple of scaredy cats. McKay can't catch us — he's just a mean old man," sneered Toad.

"And," interrupted Rooster, "he has too much honey anyway. He can't use it all himself and I want some. But if you two are too scared to come with us . . . . "

Johnny was ashamed at the memory of what he had said to the boys — "If Mr. McKay is so selfish he won't even give us some honeycomb, then I say let's go take some! C'mon Silas!"

Silas really didn't want to go steal from the beekeeper either, but as often happens when boys get together, he joined the others anyway.

The four boys made their way across summery fields filled with wildflowers to Worthy McKay's. By the time they were halfway there, they had all begun to believe that somehow they **deserved** this honey and that it was McKay's fault they didn't have any.

When they could see his buildings in the distance,

they crouched down to see if Mr. McKay was anywhere nearby. They could see the honey house, actually just a crudely built wooden shack where he removed the honey from his hives, put it in jars and did basic repairs to his hives. His house was thirty or forty yards away. It, too, was not much of a structure with its crudely built, sagging roof, even some holes in the wooden porch.

Silas wondered how Worthy walked across the porch without putting a foot through the floor, it was so rotted. He got an image of Worthy jumping from good spot to good spot like he and Johnny jumped from stone to stone across the creek.

Silas began to smile, but then realized Worthy was an old man, not a kid. He looked uneasily at his cousin. He was beginning to feel a little guilty.

Johnny, too, began to feel his bravado wearing off and knew what they were about to do was wrong. But he couldn't bring himself to go against his friends. Instead, he let them do the thinking and Johnny did just what they did. So did Silas.

When they didn't see any movement around any of the buildings, they began to creep forward, trying to be quiet. They got to the corner of the honey house and listened for any sound of Worthy McKay working.

They heard nothing so they went to the door of the honey house and walked in quickly. It took a moment for their eyes to adjust to the darkness of the shack. Rooster and Toad moved toward the workbench while Silas and Johnny waited by the door. Suddenly they felt a spooky presence and turned toward the darkest corner of the shack.

"What do you want?" Worthy McKay growled in a deep, angry voice. His weathered, craggy face caught all of the shadowy light thrown in the room and looked particularly frightening.

All four boys were startled, but no one was more scared than Johnny. Suddenly, Rooster grabbed one of the frames full of honey in the wax combs made by the bees. He lifted it up over his head and smashed it down on the workbench.

CRASH! The sound echoed in Johnny's ears. He remembered much too clearly the sight of Rooster and Toad stuffing their mouths with the honeycombs, all the while laughing at Worthy McKay standing silently, fists opening and closing at his sides, seething with anger at the boys' actions.

Looking back, Johnny realized McKay could have stopped the two boys from the damage they did. Why he didn't remains a mystery.

As Rooster and Toad ran out of the shack holding as much honey as they could carry, Johnny and Silas stayed rooted to the floor with fear. They had expected this escapade to be more like picking an apple off of someone's tree; instead it was cruel, unnecessary violence against one of their neighbors.

Granted, Worthy McKay was not very friendly to anyone and had a particular dislike of children, but he never hurt anyone and he was, after all, one of their neighbors.

By the time Johnny and Silas moved toward the door, so did the beekeeper. Worthy McKay, shaking with anger, lurched toward the boys, grabbed each of them by the collar and held them tightly, dragging them to the door of the honey house.

The boys didn't know exactly what he had in mind, but knew they did not want to stick around to find out. Two strong boys, filled with terror, was more than McKay could handle and they wrenched themselves out of his grasp. As they ran across the field, they heard him yell after them, "Don't you worry, I know who you are and I'll get you for this!"

The boys ran all the way home faster than jackrabbits in coyote country and didn't stop until they closed the barn door behind them at Johnny's. When they were able to catch their breath again and the enormity of what happened dawned on them, they really began to worry.

"My ma and pa have told me and told me that

Rooster and Toad have a mean streak. I didn't believe them, though. Do you think McKay is going to tell our folks?" asked Silas nervously.

"I don't know," Johnny answered. "But if he does, they're going to cut a switch for me, that's for sure. They've told me not to play with them."

Johnny remembers not eating much for the next couple of days. His stomach turned somersaults whenever he heard voices in the yard, sure it was Worthy McKay come for his revenge. However, after a week went by and nothing was said about the incident, Johnny began to relax. Before long, he and Silas put it out of their heads, but were determined to stay away from Rooster and Toad. And after that adventure, they both realized there were worse things than being called "chicken!"

CHAPTER 7

Look Around the Orchard

Johnny awoke from his daydream to hear his father still talking about bees." I decided to deal with McKay this year since it was so much trouble last year taking care of those bees. I know we can't pollinate the trees without them, but they are a bother. Remember when I almost tipped that hive over? And the time I forgot to tie up the ankles of my pants and those bees climbed up my leg?" reminisced James.

Johnny remembered it very well. His father was running around the yard like a mad man with his beekeeper's costume on. It was silly enough just with that big floppy hat with netting covering his face and neck. He looked like Widow Winston dressed for church — he was even wearing gloves.

That's why it was probably good his father decided to get a professional beekeeper — even if it had to be Worthy McKay.

His father continued, "We also need to check the trees for bugs and disease starting in April. We'll have to mow the orchard grass in May and then again in that dreadful August heat. And that's in addition to our other chores."

Johnny looked at his father wearily and said, "I'm tired just thinkin' about it. I'm glad you know what to do and when to do it. It seems complicated."

"Not really. It's pretty logical. Just think about the season you're in and look around the orchard. It tells you what you need to do for it," replied his father.

A swirl of color caught Johnny's eye. His mother was coming toward them, her long flowered skirt blown by the wind. It was twisting around her ankles, making it difficult to walk. His father laughed to see her grabbing and tugging at her dress with every step she took.

"Hey, Ruthie, havin' a little problem there?"

"Well, if you think it's so funny, maybe I'll take these sandwiches to someone else!" Just then a huge gust of wind caught the basket she was carrying. Instead of letting lunch go flying away, she held on tight. The force swung her around in a circle.

Astonished, James took the basket from her. "Here, don't fly away without giving us our lunch!" The three of them began giggling and then started laughing harder when Ruth's bonnet ties started beating her in the face. As she was trying to tuck them in better, she had to wrestle with her dress again. It was tangling around her legs. Finally, she was laughing so hard, she just sat down, tucking her dress tightly under her legs.

"Whew! It's so windy out here, it's gonna scatter the days of the week. We're not going to find Tuesday till next Saturday morning. How do you two get anything done out here in this wind?"

Johnny said, "Well, for one thing, we don't wear dresses!"

As James began hunting through the basket for their lunch, he said, "Ruth, look at the job Johnny did trimming these new trees. He really understands what they need."

Ruth inspected the seedling Johnny handed her. "You

did this? It looks perfect." She smiled and handed it back to Johnny. "But *you're* going to plant them, aren't you, James?" she asked worriedly.

Johnny looked questioningly at his father. His mother made it sound like the trimming wasn't very important.

"Well . . ." James began.

"Did I say something wrong? I didn't mean . . . I just meant . . ." Ruth didn't know what to say. She didn't want to hurt her son's pride, or take away anything of his accomplishment, but the actual planting in the ground was the most crucial part of the entire operation. If it was done wrong, the new trees would die.

"I was going to teach Johnny how to do the planting this year, Ruth. But don't worry. I'll be right here with him. The trimming was just a little test for him. I know he's ready to do the planting, too. Besides, I want my grandkids to enjoy these trees. Johnny won't let us down!"

Ruth and Johnny smiled. James reminded them — more times than they could count — about his future grandkids enjoying the orchard. It was a constant joke at their house, whenever he spoke about the orchard. Sometimes they bet each other how many sentences James could utter before mentioning these not-born-yet grandchildren of his. His record was five.

Johnny looked proudly at his father, then at his mother. She said, "I didn't mean you wouldn't do a good job, Johnny. I have to be reminded sometimes how old you really are. I guess that's the problem with firstborn children. We never notice how grown up and capable they really are!"

Ruth pulled her son close and gave him a hug. "Of course you'll do the planting this year. Just be sure to watch and listen and remember everything your father tells you. What you do to these trees today will be important to our orchard forever. If you do a good job, these seedlings will become strong apple trees full of apples in ten years. If you do a bad job, we won't know it until it's too late for planting and we'll lose a year of growing time."

Johnny hadn't thought of it like that. Ten years was too far away to think about. But now he knew how important this job was. "I **will** do a great job!" he vowed to himself. "This will be the best orchard in Virginia."

Even one year was too far away for a twelve-year-old to think about. If only Johnny — and all the Jackmans — could know just how different their lives will be in one year.

Chapter 8

Lambs Born

S am Jackman, James' older brother, was down the road working, too. He raised sheep for wool and some of his ewes were getting ready for birthing. The ewes seemed ready to have their lambs; they'd been gestating for about four and a half months. During this time, they needed extra food and water, plenty of exercise and good shelter through the winter.

"Silas!" Sam called for his son. "Silas! Come here!"

Silas ran over to his father, brushing his straight dark hair out of his eyes. "You need me, Pa?" he asked, eager to help.

"Yes, I need you to do a couple of things. You need to clear the pond of weeds sometime today. Otherwise it's going to foul the water and make the sheep sick. It should only take you an hour or so, but I don't want you putting it off. It's important and I need to know I can count on you. Do you understand?" Sam looked his son in the eyes.

Silas nodded.

Sam continued, "Also, I can't find a couple of the

ewes. Sometimes they wander off when they're ready to give birth. I want you to go find them. I'm going to stick close by here because it seems these three are ready any time. None of them ate anything yesterday or today," his father explained. "That's a sure sign."

Silas climbed the fence and ran off into the pasture with Macintosh, their white and brown Welsh Corgi right on his heels. Some people laugh when they're told that "Tosh" is their sheepdog, with her impossibly short legs and her long funny body, but when they see her in action, they know she's the best. She can make the sheep do exactly what Sam wants.

Sam and Tosh have some one-word commands and some hand signals and whistles worked out, but mostly Tosh just does what Sam wants before he even *knows* what he wants.

"Where are they, Tosh?" Silas wondered aloud. "Go find them!"

Tosh took off at a full clip to the east and Silas tried his best to keep up. "If only this wind was at my back, maybe it would push me along," he thought. It was about all he could do to keep Tosh in sight.

Silas ran for a while, but then had to stop. He looked at Tosh, just a speck in the distance, then bent at the waist. He put his hands on both knees and tried to breathe. He hoped Tosh knew what she was doing and wasn't just out for a run.

When he could actually fill his lungs with air again and the pounding in his chest began to slow, he stood up and listened. As the wind calmed momentarily, he heard the bleating of a sheep, probably one of the ones he was looking for.

But where was she? He looked around yet saw nothing. As he turned, though, he saw a clump of scrub oak twenty yards away. Knowing that new mothers want protection for their young, he hurried over to it. Kneeling down, he lifted some of the branches out of the way. There he found her with two newborn lambs. She had already licked them clean and they were nursing.

"Awww, how sweet!" he gushed, then looked around to make sure no one heard him.

Silas felt silly getting all mushy over a couple of cute lambs so he stood up and brushed off his pants. He knew they'd be perfectly fine right where they were; there was no reason to get them back to the barn right now. Besides, he still needed to find the other one.

He looked over the hilly pasture for Tosh but couldn't find her. He whistled the special "come-here-right-away" whistle she always responded to. This time was no exception. She came running over the hill, then stopped in her tracks as soon as she saw Silas. Tosh began to bark with urgency.

"Uh oh," thought Silas. "That doesn't sound good."

Tosh knew her barking scared the sheep so she only did it if real trouble was eminent.

Silas started to run to her. When he had almost reached her, she ran away, turning her head constantly to make sure he was following. Silas' lungs were bursting and he didn't think he could go much further over these impossible hills. He knew, though, that Tosh was serious so he tried his best to keep up.

When Tosh finally stopped, Silas was bent over in pain from the stitch in his side. But then he realized why Tosh was so worried. He saw a newborn lying next to the ewe. She was licking and licking her lamb but the lamb was not responding.

Ignoring the pain in his side, Silas grabbed the lamb and began running with it back to the farmyard. The ewe struggled to her feet to follow. Tosh knew that Silas could help the newborn so she stayed with the mother, barking occasionally to urge her to get back to the barn more quickly.

When Silas got within shouting distance of the barn, he did just that. Both his father and mother came running. When he reached them, Silas said breathlessly, "Tosh . . . . found them . . . . in the far pasture . . . . She's bringing . . . .

the ewe home now," and handed the lamb to his father.

Sam carried the lamb into the barn and laid it on some burlap bags lying in the corner. He stuck his finger in the lamb's mouth and said, "It's cold. We're going to lose this one if we don't hurry!"

He pulled one of the burlaps out from under the pathetic little lamb and began rubbing it vigorously with it. The lamb began moving a little and Sam kept at it. Just then, Tosh ushered the ewe into the barn. The exhausted mother didn't know what to do, but the humans did.

While Sam kept rubbing the lamb, Hanna brought the ewe over and pushed her close to the baby. Hanna was encouraging the baby to nurse, knowing that the first milk, the colostrum, was the most nutritious and the best thing for the lamb right then. Finally, after an agonizing wait, the lamb was able to lift its head and begin to nurse.

Both the ewe and the lamb seemed surprised at the calm that descended in the barn. Sam sat back on his heels and took a deep breath. A small tear trickled down Hanna's cheek. "I've seen this happen how many times now? And I still get all choked up when we save one."

Silas realized he had been holding his breath and let out a big sigh. "Well, I've *never* seen this happen and I don't know how you knew what to do! I thought this baby was a goner."

"There's a lot we've learned along the way in taking care of these sheep. The most important thing is that sheep tell us what's wrong if we let them. By sticking a finger in a sheep's mouth we can tell if it's healthy. The mouth should be warm. If it's cold, we need to do something. If we're lucky, like today, we know what the 'something' is. I was just hopin' her circulation was off a little. Because this was the ewe's first time havin' a baby, she may not have known quite what to do. We're just lucky you got her here so quickly and that Tosh was smart enough to get momma back here right away. Even if the lamb *was* okay, the ewe might not have bonded with it if it didn't nurse right away," Sam explained.

"Well, you make it seem so easy, Pa. I'm glad you were here and not gone to town or something," Silas said admiringly.

"Hey, did you get a chance to get the weeds and muck out of the pond?" Sam asked his son.

Silas clapped a hand to his forehead. "Oh no, I didn't! With all the excitement I completely forgot! I'll do it tomorrow," he promised.

His father looked at him sternly. "I understand that it got a little hectic today, but see you don't forget that chore tomorrow. A wise man once said 'Never put off till tomorrow what you can do today.' I think you oughta give that a try. You have a bad habit of procrastination that's only going to get you into trouble."

If Silas could only have known how right his father would be, he would have run out and taken care of the pond this minute. It would have saved him a lot of grief.

They were all looking at the newborn nursing hungrily. The ewe looked up at them, then at Tosh sitting next to her. The ewe reached up with her sticky tongue and licked Tosh right on her nose. Tosh backed up so quickly, she tripped over her own feet, embarrassed at the laughter directed her way.

"I know we don't usually go namin' all these sheep, but I think this one we should call 'Lucky,'" announced Silas.

"That she is, son, and so are we."

Chapter 9

Setting the Hives

Summer was filled with back-breaking work in the orchard and around the farm. Johnny couldn't keep up with his father who took advantage of every waking moment to work. Johnny would much rather go fishing or swimming or sit, lost in a book, in the cool shade of the huge sycamore tree in the yard.

Worthy McKay brought out his hives and Johnny kept as much distance from McKay as he could. He wasn't afraid of the bees, but he was indeed afraid of Worthy McKay. Johnny was unsure when — or if — he was going to get caught for his role in the vandalism at the honey house. He thought it best to keep a low profile when Worthy was tending to his bees.

He watched from around the corner of the barn while Worthy and his father set up the hives. They looked like dresser drawers stacked one on top of the other until they created a large rectangle made out of unpainted wood.

Johnny watched Worthy squint into the sun until he determined which was east, then he began to set up some rocks and pieces of wood. When he was satisfied, he grunted and motioned to James to help him lift the hives onto the raised platform he made. When James tried to put the hive facing south, Worthy gave him a withering look. Sheepishly, James turned the hive so it faced east.

Worthy moved very slowly and deliberately around the hives. Johnny thought it was because he was old until he heard Worthy snap at his father, "Gosh darn it, James! Would you slow down — you're scaring them! If you're not careful, you'll be getting us both stung. Or didn't you learn your lesson last year?"

Johnny giggled to hear his father get reprimanded — usually he was on the giving end.

James helped Worthy pull out each frame — Johnny counted five they'd finished and it looked like there were about the same number left — that made up the big rect-angle. They would gently brush the bees off, inspect each one, then slide them back in. Johnny had a million questions about what they were doing, but could not bring himself to go close to them. Even if he wasn't trying to keep away from Worthy McKay, he probably would not ask any questions anyway. Worthy was a man of few words and those he spoke were usually cross. Johnny also knew he didn't like people very much and he liked children even less.

Nevertheless, more and more he regretted his decision to join his so-called friends, Rooster and Toad, when they suggested going to the honey house that day. He ruefully remembered all the times his parents warned him that every decision had a consequence, whether good or bad. This was definitely one of the bad ones.

Finally, the two men finished setting up the hives. Ignoring James' invitation for a tall cold glass of lemonade, Worthy walked away, calling over his shoulder, "I'll be back in a couple weeks to check 'em. And don't you or those pesky children be messin' with them, either!"

Johnny watched his father shake his head and laugh as Worthy McKay walked out of the orchard. "Okay, Worthy, I'll see you in a couple of weeks," he called after the old man.

Running to his father from his hiding place, Johnny said, "That Worthy sure doesn't get along with people, does he?"

"No, he sure doesn't, son. But that's probably because . . . ah, well, never mind."

"What?! Why doesn't he like people? You gotta tell me, Pa. You can't just say something and not tell a guy the whole story . . . it's just not fair!" Johnny really wanted to know the secret about Worthy McKay.

His Pa laughed. "Oh, alright. I'll tell you. I guess it wouldn't hurt you to know. Back when Worthy and his wife moved here to Hadley — gosh, it must be about thirty years now — they had some hard times. See, he was making a fresh start here with a new bride and new farm. But soon after they got here, his wife had a baby."

Seeing the puzzled look on Johnny's face, James nodded. "Yep, it's true. Worthy used to be young and in love. But during the baby's birth — it was a baby boy, I think — there were problems and both the baby and Mrs. McKay died. Worthy was beside himself with grief. The neighbors tried to help, but he isn't the kind of man who wants any help. It was really his wife who made their few friends in the short time she was here. So, he never got over that. He withdrew into himself, worked hard on his farm until that got to be too much, then started with the bees. Beekeeping is a little bit easier on an old man than farming," James explained.

After mulling it over for a couple of minutes, Johnny said, "That's sad."

Now Johnny felt really bad. Worthy McKay was just a sad old man whose entire family died. He and his friends had selfishly made his life more difficult.

"Look at us standing here talking like a bunch of women when there's work to be done!" James had a twinkle in his eye when Johnny looked up at him. His mother would be furious if she had heard him say that. Johnny could hear her now — "You and that brother of yours gossip all the time! Don't you tell me it's women that gossip . . . we're too busy taking care of you to have any time to sneeze, let alone gossip!"

James and Johnny laughed, knowing that James wouldn't have said that if Ruth was in earshot.

"Let's get to work on the apple cellar, son."

Ugh. Johnny could think of nothing worse than working on the apple cellar. He believed getting stung by the thousands of bees in the beehives would be better than having to haul heavy stones to build walls for the apple cellar. But he was smart enough not to say that to his father. Instead he said, "Sure, okay, Pa!"

CHAPTER 10

Letter From Martha

It seemed to Johnny that all they did that summer was build the underground apple cellar. They worked on it whenever they had a moment free from other chores around the orchard or when they weren't helping out with Sam's sheep.

If it was just building the walls, Johnny wouldn't dislike the chore so much. But before they could build anything, they had to find the stones they'd use then haul them over. Of course, there were no stones near where they were building the apple cellar.

"Why exactly did you decide this apple cellar needed to be sixty feet long by forty feet wide?" Johnny complained one particularly difficult day. They had been lifting and carrying stones since sunup. "Lunch" meant stopping for ten minutes to eat a sandwich and have a long drink of water.

"Because I never want to do this again and this one should serve us the rest of our time here on the farm. I don't see why you're complaining, anyway. I was the one who dug this out one shovelful at a time." James was annoyed at his son. Hard work never hurt anyone. And where was his pride in doing a job well?

"It wasn't my fault I was too young to help!" As soon as the words were out, Johnny wanted them back. He could get the strap for talking back to his father.

When James didn't respond, Johnny felt a twinge of guilt. The way his father had been working today, he probably wouldn't have the energy to punish him. And, of course, his father was right. Johnny didn't help dig out the cellar at all. James dug every shovelful of dirt out of there by himself. Just an inch deep out of an area sixty by forty would be a job, but James had shoveled it all to a depth of about five feet. He even made stairs out of the earth at one end.

This cellar has been a work-in-progress for several years now. Since they only work on it when the other chores are done — and there are LOTS of other chores — they don't work on the apple cellar often. His father works much harder than Johnny does and doesn't complain at all. He does, however, need Ruth to rub liniment on his shoulders and back when he overdoes it.

Watching his father strain and stretch and push and lift, Johnny got a burst of energy. It's wonderful what guilt can do for a person!

They worked in silence for a while, building the wall with the rocks they collected before lunch. The sun was hot and the sweat was pouring off their necks and backs. Their shirts were wet enough they could have wrung them out like a dishcloth.

Johnny was tired of working but didn't dare say anything to his father. Little did he know his father was desperately trying to think of a chore — any chore — that needed to be done so he wouldn't have to work on the wall any longer. Luck was with them that day when they saw Sam walking up carrying something in his shirt pocket.

"Nice of you to show up to help us today!" James

called sarcastically to his brother.

"What! And get this pretty face all sweaty and dirty like yours?" Sam wrinkled his nose in disgust. "Whew! You two are not smelling like roses today!"

"Yeah, yeah, yeah. Did you just come to bother us?" James was quite glad to have the excuse to sit down on part of the wall already built. As he looked around, he was surprised to see they were almost halfway finished. Then only the roof would be left . . .

"I realize you're probably too busy to stop and read this so I'll just take it into the house and give it to Ruthie," teased Sam, beginning to walk toward the house.

Normally James would have wrestled it out of his hands like when they were boys, but he was beyond tired and could only sit. "Get over here you old fool and tell me why you're here."

Sam looked at his brother with fake pity. "Oh, alright. You are so pathetic," then turning to Johnny he said, "Make sure you help him back to the house tonight. Otherwise he'll have to spend the night out here. It's a good thing he already built the stairs — I'm not sure he could jump up over the wall."

James smiled weakly and stuck out his hand. Sam deposited a letter from their sister Martha into it. "She wrote about their plans to come from Atlanta for their Christmas visit."

James let the letter rest on his hand. "Will you read it to me?" he asked in his most pathetic voice. Sam stared at him until James could look pathetic no longer. They both broke into big bellylaughs until Sam picked up the letter.

"I really am pooped," said James. "You should be a lot nicer to me."

"Can you believe this old man, Johnny? I'll just start calling him 'Grandpa,' " said Sam as he began to take the letter from their little sister out of its envelope.

Dear Sam and Hanna, James and Ruth,

I hope this letter finds you and the children all well and happy.

We are all very excited here in Atlanta about our trip to Hadley at Christmastime. I wanted to let you know our plans. William and I are going to meet up with Victoria and Robert in Charlotte, North Carolina, then take the train together to Hadley. We figure that four adults can keep five children happy for the time we'll be traveling!

Victoria and I are looking forward to reminiscing about growing up with all of you boys in Hadley. And how you tortured us with the frogs and snakes you always brought home from the pond. That will give our husbands a chance to talk together about their problems with their plantations. I declare I never realized how hard it is to run these big places — I thought having slaves take care of it all meant it would be easy.

My Billy and the twins are looking forward to meeting their cousins. They've never met any of you. Since Billy is only seven, and Lucy and Loreen only five, they weren't even born when we came back to Hadley the last time. That was nine years ago when Pa died. I often regret that we moved so far away that we can hardly ever see each other.

I think Victoria feels the same way. I had a letter from her recently. She told me that she overheard her girls when they were playing. It seems Rebecca (who's ten) and Sissy (who's nine) were talking about families. Rebecca said to her sister, "I wish I was part of Mammy's family." (Mammy is the slave who takes care of the girls.) When Sissy asked her why, Rebecca told her, "They just have so much fun together — there's so many of them!"

Well, it just about broke Vic's heart because, as you know, there's so many of us! But the children don't realize it since we never see each other. So, we're both determined — no matter what happens — to bring our families to Hadley. So get ready . . . it will be wild.

I'm not sure about the sleeping arrangements, but it

would seem that we could stay at one house, while Victoria, Robert and the girls can stay at the other. So you figure that out.

I can't think of what else to tell you, except that we're all so looking forward to seeing everyone.

Have you heard from Frank or is he on the trail somewhere? And we're hoping that Thomas can get away from Philadelphia and that blacksmith shop of his to join us. I had a letter from him over a year ago, so I don't know if he's planning on joining us for Christmas or not.

I did hear from Charles in Baltimore, though. It sounded like he will be able to come to Hadley, but that's about all he said in his letter, other than his family is doing fine.

But I'll end this letter now. I'm keeping my fingers crossed that everything works out for all of us to be together this Christmas.

Love,
Martha

The sweaty exhausted workers used Martha's letter as an excuse to be done with the apple cellar for the day. And, as luck would have it, they didn't get a chance to do much more work on it the rest of the summer.

Before they knew it, summer was over, Worthy McKay had put the bees to bed for the winter and it was time to get ready for the holidays.

CHAPTER **11**

Christmas Preparations, 1860

E ven though Sam and James didn't get to see their brothers and sisters very often, all their arrangements to come to Hadley for Christmas 1860 seemed to pay off. Everyone was excited about the family holiday party; it was the first time everyone was together since Pa's funeral, nine years earlier. Getting the whole clan together was cause for celebration.

Samuel and James took Silas and Johnny hunting early one December morning, hoping to find wild turkeys, rabbits and deer. It snowed lightly during the night, which meant fresh snow on the ground. It had been so cold the last few days, the men were afraid they wouldn't find many animals. They were happily surprised that their problem wasn't finding the animals; it was trying to follow just one set of tracks. They saw animals all over the woods and not hiding like they normally do.

Silas and Johnny had only been allowed to hunt with their fathers on two previous occasions. Their fathers had carried the guns and handled the loading each time, but did let the boys actually fire at a few rabbits. They missed each one, though.

Their main job on those early hunting trips was to learn how to remain safe and how to keep others safe. Only then did they learn the next step in hunting, how to track the animals. After that, they'd be able to learn how to load the rifles and practice shooting. When the boys were just youngsters, their fathers taught them how to read the animal tracks and distinguish one animal from the next. Often this was one of the games the boys would play on their own in the woods or down by the river. It was much more difficult when they didn't have the guidance of their fathers, however. They couldn't imagine ever knowing as much about hunting as their fathers did.

The women and girls were at Ruth's house, busily making gifts for everyone. They were knitting warm wool scarves for all the men and boys and making aprons for all the women and girls. They were working on each others' aprons in secret, trying to outdo each other by stitching their most intricate embroidery. Elizabeth, Lydia and Mary, especially, wanted to impress their mothers with how much they've learned. Little Emily and Abigail had to be content playing with the pieces of lace and ribbon that fell to the floor. Eventually they gathered up enough in their chubby little fingers to give their dolls little napkins and tablecloths for a miniature tea party.

They were also making Christmas decorations for the house and delicious holiday treats to eat. While their mothers were busy in the kitchen, all the girls were busy making paper chains. Lydia, being the oldest girl, designated herself "Queen of the Scissors" and was the one cutting the strips of colored paper. The other girls, pasting the strips together, became her loyal subjects who, of course, had to do exactly what she told them.

"No, no, no! Don't put the blue one on the green one! That looks awful." she demanded. When she saw Elizabeth's lip quiver like she might start crying, Lydia used a silly squeaky voice and said, "As your Queen, I decree blue must always go on a yellow one."

Everyone laughed and the mothers came out to see what all the noise was. When they saw how long the paper chain already was and all the strips of paper that had yet to be pasted on, they teased the girls, saying, "We asked you to make decorations for the house, not the whole town."

When the girls finished the paper chain, Lydia figured they had enough to loop around the main rooms of both her house and her cousins' house as well as to decorate the tree her father was going to cut down soon. They had decided that Uncle Charles' family and Uncle Thomas' family would stay with James and Ruth during the big holiday visit, and that Aunt Victoria's family and Aunt Martha's family would stay with Sam and Hanna. Uncle Frank, because he was by himself and because all the kids wanted him at their own houses, would alternate between both. Christmas dinner would be at James and Ruth's house.

The girls called to their mothers to come look at their enormous paper chain. After they hung it around the room and got the other half ready to take to Elizabeth and Abigail's house, Mary went to the kitchen to bring out the popped corn to string for the tree. Mostly they snacked on it, but some of it found its way on to their needles. When they finished, they again called their mothers to come look at their handiwork.

Hanna laughed when she saw their popcorn string. "Why is it that your paper chain can go from here to Boston, but your popcorn chain will barely wrap around the Christmas tree!"

"I guess it's good that they ate the popcorn and not the colored paper. It shows they have good taste," Ruth teased. "But now we have to clean up this mess. The boys will be back soon and we'll need to help with whatever they managed to bring home."

Chapter 12

Hunting Christmas Dinner

The boys and their fathers had been looking forward to this hunting trip, but for different reasons.

The boys felt excited because they had been promised they could do some actual hunting this time, assuming they could first answer their fathers' questions about safety and tracking. Sam and James looked forward to this trip because they had seen lots of animal tracks. They had high expectations of bringing home plenty of meat for the big Christmas gathering, and maybe even for the rest of the winter. Hunting in the winter was not particularly enjoyable — it's cold, most of the animals are nestled away for the winter, and there is less daylight so they had to take more time away from their everyday chores.

As they were walking, Sam commented, "I'm glad to see you boys remembered to walk shoulder to shoulder rather than single file while we were out today."

Silas replied, "Yes, sir, we don't want either of you slipping in the snow and shooting us in the back on our first real hunting trip."

The boys laughed, but their fathers didn't. "Staying safe isn't a joke, boys," said James sternly. "If you don't take this seriously, then we'll know you aren't ready."

"No, we're ready . . . we do take it seriously . . . no more jokes . . . we promise." the boys both stammered, talking over each other.

"Okay, just remember that."

They walked through the woods silently, looking for tracks in the snow. Presently Sam said, "This is a good place to load the guns, eh, James?" Looking at the boys' confusion, he explained, "You're right. Normally the gun is always loaded because, well, let's face it, when you need it, you need it now, and if it's not loaded, it doesn't do you much good. But for our trip today, we thought it might be better to teach you how to load these out here. Away from the house."

The boys looked a little sheepish. So their own fathers didn't trust them to load a gun. Well, we'll show them, they both thought.

The men stood the rifles in front of them. James began. "We'll show you once, so pay very close attention. You never want to waste your powder. You put this much powder here into the barrel. Then you put this much lead into this piece of cloth and put it in the barrel. Then you get your ramrod from under the gun here and ram it all down. Not only does this speed up your loading, but when it's shot, that little piece of cloth helps clear the barrel of the powder from the previous shot. Then you put a few grains of powder into the pan of the flintlock here and you're ready. We are able to reload in about thirty seconds, but we've been doing it longer. It takes practice to reload quickly."

"You'll be able to hit your target best between sixty and a hundred yards," continued Sam. "Don't even try beyond that, because these rifles aren't made for more distance. Now you try."

Silas and Johnny both reached for their fathers' rifles. James pulled his away from Johnny with a stern look. "This one is already loaded. You must *always* know whether your gun is loaded or not. If you can't remember if it's loaded, there's a way to check. You take the ramrod and run it inside the barrel. Then measure how far it goes against the length of the barrel. If there's something blocking it, it won't go all the way down. If you put another charge into your gun, it can burst and take off your fingers, your hand . . . or worse," he added ominously.

Sam nodded his head solemnly, "Also, if there are any sparks left after you shoot, reloading can make a premature explosion."

Seeing the boys' pale faces, James reassured them by saying, "Yes, these things can happen. But no, they probably won't if you take care and remember."

Suddenly, the boys weren't nearly as excited about hunting. In fact, they felt quite scared. There was a lot to know about guns and hunting.

After Silas loaded Sam's gun, he said, "Why don't you boys carry these now," and he handed his rifle back to Silas. James handed his to Johnny.

The Jackmans didn't have much money for frivolous things, but they did spend some of their hard-earned money on good rifles. Accordingly, they took very good care of their guns. They cleaned them every time they used them and put them in places of honor above the fireplaces in their homes. Not only were they safe there, they were also ready whenever they were needed.

After years of watching their fathers handle their guns, both boys understood that their families' survival depended on these guns. Not only for food, but for protection also. They also began to understand how dangerous these rifles could be.

Walking a little further, they came upon an area

covered with animal tracks.

"Hmm, must be a game trail," Sam said, pointing ahead.

"Johnny, why does your Uncle Sam think that?" quizzed James.

Without hesitation, Johnny answered, "Because all these tracks seem to be going to and from the same place. Maybe there's a stream down that way where they all go. This is like a crossroads for the animals."

"Very good. You've been paying attention," smiled his father. "Anything you want to add, Silas?"

"Well, it looks like that's a turkey . . . and there are some rabbit tracks . . . and that's . . . a squirrel?" said Silas, pointing.

Sam beamed at his son. "You got 'em all." Sam paused, looking at the ground nearby. "How 'bout that one?" he asked, pointing.

"White tailed deer," both boys shouted at once.

"Hey, pipe down. Do you want to scare everything away? Then we'll only get porridge for Christmas dinner," complained James.

They decided to follow the deer tracks. As they were walking, Johnny admired the gun in his hand, letting his mind wander. "I'd like to shoot a bear," he said matter-of-factly. "Yes, definitely a bear."

His father laughed. "For someone who hasn't hunted much, that's pretty confident thinking. Unfortunately, all the bears are bedded down for the winter."

They began to see more sign of deer so they knew that deer were close. All four of the hunters stood as silently as they could be so they wouldn't scare them away.

Suddenly there was a rustling in the brush ahead of them. They all looked in that direction expecting to see the deer they'd been tracking. Instead, what they saw stopped their hearts.

Looming ahead was a female black bear standing on

her hind legs. She let out a loud snarl and began lumbering toward them. Standing, she was over five and a half feet tall. Her thick black coat made her appear even bigger than she really was, yet her face was deceptively dainty — almost as if it were perched on the wrong body. Until her lip curled over her sharp yellow teeth, that is.

The boys, frozen with fear, forgot they were carrying the guns. James, who was standing between the boys, grabbed the rifle from Johnny and took aim. Silas recovered from the surprise and lifted his gun to his shoulder. In his haste to fire, though, he knocked into James, forcing him to shoot above the bear's head.

Now the bear came faster and James had to reload. Even though James could reload in thirty seconds, they didn't have that much time. The bear was close and getting closer . . . fast. Silas knew he had one shot at this powerful animal headed straight for his Uncle James. It was as if the bear knew James had tried for the first shot and she was going to teach him a lesson. Silas also knew there was no way he would ever be able to reload his gun at all with a bear in his face. He lifted his gun to his shoulder again, took aim and pulled the trigger, expecting the bear to fall to the ground. Instead, the bear let out a howl of pain but kept charging. Now even faster.

"You only winged him! Reload!" yelled Sam.

By then, the furious bear was just a few feet from James who was still loading his gun. When he looked up, he saw the wild look in the bear's eye. He froze.

"SHOOT IT!" he heard, and James raised the rifle to his shoulder. He pulled the trigger just as her front paw lifted to maul him.

BANG!

One shot to the bear's chest was all it took and the majestic animal fell. As she did so, she was still able to get a swipe at James and the razor sharp claws took a neat scratch right down his arm. He looked down and saw blood seep through his shirt.

The four hunters hadn't moved from where they stood when the bear fell. They were all panting and the boys began to shake. Sam and James looked at each other in disbelief and James began to take off his jacket to check the damage.

Johnny couldn't look at anyone, he felt such shame to have been so frightened that he couldn't even move. And Silas couldn't look at anyone because he felt this close call was his fault. If he hadn't bumped Uncle James, the bear wouldn't have come close enough to reach him.

Sam couldn't believe there was a bear roaming around in December and was ashamed for not being prepared. He knew that bears often left their dens in the winter, especially when they had cubs. As he turned and looked around in the snow behind them from the direction they came, he saw them clearly. Just off to the side. Bear tracks.

James had his shirt and coat off, and was looking at the claw marks raked down his right arm. "It's just on the skin . . . not too deep . . . there, it's not even bleeding any more. I'll be fine," he said confidently. "But this coat has seen better days. I was hoping we wouldn't have to tell the women about this, but Ruth just might notice this." He held up his coat, the right sleeve in shreds.

James looked at his hunting companions, still shocked by what had happened. "Hey, it's all right, everything's gonna be fine, we're all okay," he said soothingly to them.

Sam looked at him and said, "There's probably a cub nearby, otherwise she wouldn't have charged us like that." Shaking his head in wonder, he walked over to James and took a look at his arm. "Yeah, looks like the bleeding has stopped. Shall we go home?"

James shook his head. "Nah, we said we'd teach these boys how to hunt today so let's finish." He paused, then smiled and said, "I guess they didn't expect us to give them the final exam first, though, did they?"

When Johnny and Silas still wouldn't look at their fathers, James said softly, "There's nothing to be ashamed of here, boys. Any sane man would be scared when a bear charges him. Everything is perfectly fine — except my clothes — and we have Christmas dinner to hunt. Do you want to hunt or go home? Either choice is fine by me. Sam and I can finish up."

Silas said, "I'm sorry I bumped your arm, Uncle James."

"It was an accident. Nothin' to be sorry about," said James, putting his arm around Silas' shoulder.

"C'mon, let's go. We'll swing by here and pick up this beast on our way home. We may even have to leave her till we can get the horse out here. She's big!" commented Sam.

Johnny walked toward his father, "I . . . I . . . I was so scared I couldn't move. I'm not much of a hunter, I guess."

James stopped and put his hands on both of Johnny's shoulders. "That is not the way I want you to talk. You'd be stupid not to be scared. And I know if you really needed to, you would have done what needed to be done. But you saw we had it all under control. You and Sam were able to sit back and watch the "Silas and James Show.""

Johnny smiled. His father had a way of putting everything in perspective. What's done is done and this was James' way of getting on with things.

As they began to walk away, Johnny said, "Hey, shouldn't we reload?"

"And you said you're not much of a hunter!" smiled James.

The rest of the day was a lot less exciting, but the boys were able to successfully track and shoot three rabbits, a deer and one huge wild turkey for Christmas dinner. When they got home, James had already taken his jacket off. Telling Ruth about their close call could wait. Silas boasted, "Ma! We got tons of meat."

Johnny chimed in, "What a great day. Hey — is

dinner ready? I'm starved."

Their exhausted fathers looked at their wives and sank wearily into the closest chairs available. "Where do they get that energy? For every step I took, they probably took four, what with all their running around. I think they could go out and do it all over again right now," Sam exclaimed.

James complained, "I'm not entirely sure I'm going to be able to get out of bed in the morning. Will you feed me my dinner right here, Ruth?"

Ruth laughed at him, "You old man! All you did was get food for us and our guests — look what we've done." They dragged the tired men up out of their chairs to show them the pies, cookies, candies, cakes, breads and other goodies they made. Then the girls showed them the decorations they worked on all day.

"So you get out there and wash up. We need to get home, have dinner and do some of those chores," Hanna demanded, pulling Sam's arm.

"Ok, ok, I'm going," Sam grumbled, pretending to fall asleep as he was walking. When he got to where Mary was standing, he leaned over and rested his chin on the top of her head, giving a loud pretend snore.

"Oh, Uncle Sam," she giggled and moved out from under him. He pretended to stumble all the way to the front door, where he grabbed his hat from the table and waved it behind him as a farewell. Everyone laughed and Silas and Johnny rolled their eyes at each other as if to say, "How can a grown man act so silly?"

After they had gone, Lydia said, "Are you going to cut down the Christmas tree now, Daddy?"

James looked at her with weary eyes and said, "Your Uncle Sam was pretending, but that really is how I feel. Can it wait a few days? I need some sleep."

Mary looked at her father with big eyes. "Are you really going to sleep for a few *days*?"

Her mother said, "No, honey, but the tree can wait. We'll all go to find one on Christmas Eve, after everyone is here. Let's have dinner now."

Turning to James, Ruth asked, "What did you bring home?"

James told her, "A white tail, some rabbits and a terrific turkey. Oh, yeah, and a bear."

Ruth turned to look at him with one eyebrow cocked.

CHAPTER 13

Christmas Eve Visitors

Finally, after waiting and waiting what seemed like forever, Christmas Eve dawned clear but cold. There hadn't been any snow for several days so no one was worried about the family getting stuck somewhere and not being able to make it for the festivities. Everyone had been told to come to James' house first.

All the children were playing outside where they could keep an eye out for travelers on the road. They hoped everyone would arrive in time to go together to pick out the Christmas tree.

The first to arrive in Hadley, around noon, were Uncle Charles and Uncle Thomas. Charles was the oldest and Thomas just one year younger. Except for the Jackman dark hair, they looked nothing alike.

Charles worked in a textile factory in Baltimore. Because he worked indoors and didn't do much physical labor, he didn't have much of a tan and had put on some weight around his middle. Thomas, however, was skinny as a rail and had huge forearms and biceps, developed in his work as a blacksmith in Philadelphia.

After all the hugs and kisses, Ruth asked, "Where is everyone else? Aren't they coming?"

Charles explained, "When I told Anne it was going to take at least twenty-one hours on the train, she suddenly remembered she promised her aunt she and the kids would spend the holidays with her." He pretended to look hurt. "But seriously, even with these new trains and railroads, it's a tough trip. It actually took twenty-eight hours — I'm glad they decided to stay put."

Thomas nodded in agreement because his wife, Laura, had second thoughts about bringing their family on the trip, too. "Just the trip from Philly to Baltimore was eleven hours. And then to come the rest of the way with him . . ." he gestured toward Charles. "That's enough to make a person not want to make the trip."

"Well," Charles retorted, "At least *I* didn't snore in *your* ear the entire trip here."

The children giggled at their uncles' playacting. But Ruth was concerned. "Are you sure that's okay? Will they spend the holiday with their families? Won't you miss them? You'll be gone a long time. Will they be okay?"

"Enough already. Everything will be fine. Anne has family near by and Laura does, too, doesn't she, Tom?" Uncle Tom nodded. "And we did decide to cut our trip a little short to get back to them sooner. But it's perfectly fine," reassured Charles.

"Not to worry," quipped Tom. "Got any food ready? I'm starved."

Everyone understood the topic was to be dropped and the women started bustling around the kitchen getting sandwiches for the hungry travelers.

Changing the subject, Charles said, "Hey, we came through Harpers Ferry on the way here. I've been wanting to see it ever since I read about John Brown in the paper. I don't get to many famous places, after all," he joked.

James said, "Refresh my memory, I don't always get the chance to read the paper. Some of us work for a living . . . not like you city folk."

"Ha, ha, ha, very funny," snorted Charles. "Okay, listen and learn from your big brother. John Brown got about twenty men together and captured some prominent people in town, then held them hostage. He called himself "Isaac Smith" because everyone knew — well, everyone who reads a newspaper, that is," Charles winked at his brother, "everyone knew John Brown is a very outspoken and well-known abolitionist. That means he wants to end slavery, James . . ."

"I know what it means, you . . . you . . . "

"Now boys," cautioned Ruth, "do we have to separate you two?"

In unison, the grown 'boys' said, "No, ma'am."

Charles continued, "But it was ugly. He was captured, some of his men were killed, some escaped and some of the townspeople were killed. A jury found him guilty of treason and he was sentenced to hang. I just thought it was interesting to see the place where someone really stood up for what he believed in."

"Yes, it was good he was against slavery, but that never excuses violence. Couldn't he have made his point any other way?" asked Hanna.

"That's just what Mr. Lincoln said about the whole affair. Hanna, you could be President," Charles teased.

"Well, of course I could. But then who would make dinner?" she quipped.

Suddenly the children were shouting and the adults in the house heard hootin' and hollerin'. At the same time the women looked at each other, laughed and said, "Frank's here!"

Just then the door burst open and Frank grabbed Ruth in one arm and Hanna in the other. He twirled them both around twice, yelling, "It's *cold* here! I'm goin' back to Texas where the sun shines twenty-six hours a day!"

"Well, if you wouldn't steal two hours of our sunshine, maybe it *would* be warmer around here. Now let go of my wife!" James pretended to punch Frank in the nose to the delight of the children all gathered around their favorite uncle.

"No, Daddy, don't!" squealed Mary. "Uncle Frank's my buddy and you don't hit him."

Frank picked up six-year-old Mary and used her as a shield to protect himself. "Yeah, you big bad bully, picking on your little brother. You should be ashamed of yourself. Hey — is there any food ready? I'm starved!" Frank tossed his cowboy hat on the nearest chair.

Hanna and Ruth had just finished putting away the food they had out for Charles and Tom so they both rolled their eyes and Hanna said, "You all could have at least planned to get here at the same time so we wouldn't have to be jumping up every fifteen minutes!"

The men were worried. They thought Hanna and Ruth were serious and they didn't want the two best cooks in the world to be angry at them. Then they saw Ruth wink at Johnny, who was looking just as worried as the men.

"Ah, Ruthie, I was just jokin'. I can make my own sandwich. I do it all the time. Remember, I don't have a wife to spoil me."

Many women would jump at the chance to be Frank's wife. He was the youngest and best looking of the Jackman brothers. Working as a cowboy certainly agreed with him.

"What?!" Ruth said in mock surprise. "Let you wreck my kitchen? It's much better if I do it. But there are some socks that need mending, if you're looking for some women's work to do."

As Ruth and Hanna went to the kitchen and his brothers teased him, Frank sat down and asked, "Are the girls here yet?"

"No, but we're expectin' them real soon. The train comes in 'bout three o'clock. They should have met up in Charlotte, North Carolina, and traveled here together. Let's just hope Ruth and Hanna haven't put away all the food again by the time they get here," said Sam, winking.

Ruth bustled into the room. "I heard that. Besides, I'm not planning on feeding them till supper time, so you just better hope they get here at a decent hour or ya'll will starve!"

After Frank finished eating, he announced, "I declare! That's about the finest thing I've had to eat since I was here the last time. You just get to be better and better cooks." Then in a stage whisper, "Almost as good as our cook on the trail."

Hanna and Ruth stopped in their tracks and lowered their eyes at him. They both started speaking at once.

"You mean to sit there and tell me some man out in the middle of nowhere can cook up biscuits like this . . .

"I don't know what you're thinkin', saying the beans you get on the trail can compare with my . . ."

When everyone began to laugh at them, Hanna and Ruth realized they were being teased and started to laugh, too. "Well, just for that, Mr. Frank Jackman, you go and get our coffee," said Ruth as she plopped into a chair and put her feet up.

"I wouldn't have it any other way, your Highness," said Frank, bowing low.

Chapter 14

Uncle Frank's Story

The children burst into the room begging for Frank's attention. "Please, please, *please* tell us a story!"

They were so insistent and cute, the adults couldn't contain themselves any longer. "Yes, yes, please 'Uncle Frank' tell us a story!" They cried in high voices.

"Oh for Pete's sake, stop all that caterwaulin'. You sound like the baby cows I have to take care of on the drive." He thought for a minute then began his story.

"One time — now, this is a true story, mind ya'll — we were out in Oklahoma territory. I wasn't the boss then. In fact, it was only my third or fourth drive.

"Well, we had five or six hundred head of cattle bedded down for the night and we were sittin' around the campfire havin' one last cup of coffee and singin' one last song. I think it was that one about some yellow rose in Texas. What's that one called?"

"Would it be 'The Yellow Rose of Texas' maybe?" answered Charles sarcastically.

"Well, that it would, big brother," said Frank with a wink at the children. "Anyway, we were all bedded down, but I wasn't asleep yet when I heard the cattle start mooooo-ving around."

"Uncle Frank!" groaned Silas.

"Well, the others heard it, too, and we all got up to check it out. I thought maybe it was a pack of coyotes. But they were gettin' more and more worked up. We couldn't see much — the moon was covered by clouds. But out of the corner of my eye I saw something, then I heard the whinny of a horse and I knew it weren't no coyotes. It was rustlers! So I yelled 'Rustlers!' — since yelling 'Coyotes' wouldn't have been true — and then those daggummed rustlers started yellin' and scarin' the cattle. So who knows what cattle do when they're scared?"

Every hand in the room went up, as if it were their Sunday school teacher asking a question. Frank pointed at Lydia. She replied with eyes as big as saucers, "They stampede!"

"Yes, indeedy, little lady. That's just what they did. They went right through our camp. Those stupid cows get so terrified, they don't even think. I'm sure their little brains are just tellin' 'em 'Run! Run! Don't look where you're goin' — just squash anything in your way!'

"I don't have to tell you we all scattered like leaves in a tornado. Everyone got out just in time. No injuries to any cowboys except old Bill. After all the excitement, he tripped over a log that got kicked out of the fire. Just bruised himself, is all.

"But those crazy cows, they ran right through the chuckwagon — pushed it over and smashed it to smithereens. Food and pots and pans scattered everywhere. There was no food left to salvage. The heavy pots and pans were knocked all over and dented — one even had a perfect hoof print in the middle of it. That gives you an idea of the power behind that many cows — those pans were made of the heaviest cast iron. Heavy enough that you young 'uns couldn't even lift one by yourself."

The children looked at each other, trying to get their brains around the destruction of Uncle Frank's camp.

"And that's not even the worst of it. They trampled my bedroll to shreds. And then they were gone before we could even saddle up our horses."

"Did you get them back?" asked Johnny.

"Nope. Well, we got a few who couldn't keep up with the others, but not even enough to go on to Kansas City. We turned around and went back. And hoo-boy, did the trail boss get yelled at. I learned some lessons from that drive."

There was murmuring in the room while everyone digested that story.

"Hey! I know another story about rustlers. This friend of mine was in a saloon one night. This cowboy walks in with a paper cowboy hat, and a paper shirt, and paper pants and even paper boots. They arrested him for . . . rustling!"

The adults all laughed at Frank's joke. When they saw the puzzled looks on the kids faces, they laughed even harder. Finally, Frank explained, "Get it? Paper . . . rustling? Oh well, think about it for awhile, you'll get it. Now skeedaddle out of here. I'm tired of talkin'," and he gathered all the girls up in an enormous hug which made them all squeal and try to get away. He reached down and solemnly shook hands with Johnny and then with Silas. "And that's why," he said with a twinkle in his eye, "I absolutely forbid you to grow up to be a cowboy."

Silas said, "Aw, Uncle Frank!"

Johnny declared with equal solemnity, "And it's why I absolutely forbid you to **quit** bein' a cowboy! No one around Hadley has any great stories like that!"

CHAPTER **15**

Hurry Up and Wait

While the folks were in Hadley listening to Uncle Frank's stories, the travelers from the South were making their way to Hadley.

Martha, the youngest Jackman sister, her husband William, and their children were on the train from Atlanta to Charlotte, North Carolina where they were to meet up with Victoria's family. Martha and her children, seven-year-old Billy and five-year-old twins Lucy and Loreen, had inherited red hair like Johnny's. Little did they know how happy he'd be to see others with crazy red hair like his.

Billy and the twins were very excited at first and ran all over the train, inspecting every nook and cranny, much to the dismay of their fellow travelers. But the novelty of a new adventure soon wore off, and Lucy and Loreen began to whine from boredom.

Martha tried to get them to take a nap, but it was no use. Especially since Billy tried to keep himself occupied by seeing how many times he could poke one of his sisters without anyone noticing it was him.

His record was . . . once.

"Ma-a-a-a-a! Billy's poking me!"

"Am not!"

"Are too!"

"I saw you!"

"Enough!" Together Martha and William hissed at their children, then rolled their eyes at each other. This was going to be a very long trip.

Eighteen hours later, they reached Charlotte where Victoria and Robert were waiting.

Victoria was the sister in the middle of the family. Not only was she attractive like the rest of the Jackmans, she was also as tall as her brothers, which made her seem as stately as royalty.

After a round of hugs and introductions, Victoria said, "We almost gave up on you coming in today. We found a little boarding house nearby and got rooms for all of us. We were only going to wait another half hour for you before we headed over. The girls are sick to death of trains and train stations!"

'The girls' were Rebecca who was ten and Sissy who was nine. Both of them seemed destined to be tall like their mother.

Martha nodded. "I know exactly how they feel."

The two families arranged for their luggage to be sent over to the boarding house. Even though the weather was colder than they were used to, the boarding house wasn't too far and would give the children a change of pace. They decided to walk.

Victoria told them about their trip, which, after hearing about Martha's, didn't seem quite so bad.

"It took us about ten hours to get from Columbia here to Charlotte. We were trying to figure out when you would get here, but it's difficult because nothing is written down. Apparently there is a timetable in the newspaper, but no one bothered to tell us that. I told the Station Master he needed to get little papers printed with the times the trains arrive and depart. He told me it was a good idea and he'd look into it," Victoria boasted.

As they walked, the children behaved like monkeys escaped from the zoo. They ran around, shouting and laughing all the way to Belle's Boarding House. After trying to settle them down to no avail, the adults finally had enough. As they walked up the broad steps to the house, William said very quietly and sternly to his children and nieces, "Do not move one inch. Do not make one sound."

As he turned, he heard a giggle and whirled around with a withering look at them. The children did not move one inch or make one sound.

Belle, who had seen and heard the commotion but waited just inside, came out on the porch.

Victoria introduced them to the plump woman who owned the establishment where they were to stay the night.

"William and Martha, this is Belle . . . I'm sorry, I don't know your last name."

"Not important. It's too long and hard to pronounce anyway. It's just 'Belle.' I hope ya'll will be comfortable here. I'll go make something to eat."

As she walked away, she called over her shoulder, "Now don't you worry about those children. This house needs some noise once in awhile." She looked at the children with a jolly twinkle in her eye, still standing where they were ordered by their parents. "Ya'll make yourselves at home."

When they didn't budge, still frightened from the scolding they received, Belle stopped, then said, "Pleeeeease?" The adults looked at each other, laughed and motioned for the children to go play, which they did instantly before any parents could change their minds.

After they refreshed themselves with the food Belle provided, the parents had regained some patience. The children had spent a little of their energy playing in the yard.

But when it got too cold outside and they had to come inside, they pretty much took over the house. The children were running around, the adults were playing cards and both groups generally annoyed everyone else!

Bedtime couldn't have been more welcome. That night, they all slept soundly in the comfortable feather beds piled deep with soft, thick blankets. After a hearty breakfast and good-byes, the group made their way back to the train station.

Once they left, the guests remaining at Belle's place breathed a sigh of relief.

After a long wait at the station, their train finally arrived. The travelers now believed Belle's warning that you have to "hurry up and wait" at the train station because no one knows when the trains will arrive.

They weren't looking forward to being on the train even longer than the first leg of their journey, but they were excited about getting to Hadley for the holidays.

CHAPTER 16

More Christmas Visitors

As the children were bundling up to go outside and wait for the rest of their aunts, uncles and cousins to finally arrive, they heard noisy voices outside.

Lydia threw open the door and there stood Victoria and Martha and their families. "Whew, open up and put on the coffee! We're freezin' to death out here!" Martha shouted. They all tried to get through the door at once but the children, only halfway into their boots, mittens and scarves, were still standing in the doorway. Everyone was trying to hug everyone else and the little kids were trying to avoid getting stepped on.

Finally Charles said loudly, "Alright already. Everyone stop talkin'! Everyone who wants to hug go over there," he pointed to the far corner of the room. "Everyone who wants to go outside to play go over there," and he pointed to the other corner.

Everyone began talking again and trying to go to the proper corner but no one was succeeding. Charles began laughing and threw up his hands. "I give up! Everybody do whatever you want!"

When the travelers had hugged and taken off their coats and the noise settled down, Elizabeth asked, "Now, who are you people?" which set off gales of laughter again among the adults.

"It has been a long time since we've seen you, Elizabeth, don't pay them any mind." Victoria shot her brothers and sisters a look. "You're probably the only one with sense enough to ask! It's a shame we can't see you more often, but traveling is so difficult and takes so long. Maybe in a hundred years, families will be able to see each other more often, even if they do live far away from each other."

Victoria pulled her two girls out from where they were hiding behind her.

"So, get ready for your lesson. I'm your Aunt Victoria and this is my husband, Robert. I am your daddy's sister. Just like you are Silas' sister."

She put her hand on each blond, curly head as she introduced her daughters to cousins they'd never met.

"These are our girls, Rebecca — she's ten, and Sissy — she's nine. And this is Aunt Martha and your Uncle William. Martha is also your daddy's sister."

Martha and William stepped forward and pulled their shy children with them.

Martha took over the introductions now. "This is our son, Billy, who's seven and our twins, Lucy and Loreen. They're five. Does that about do it, honey? It looks like you and the twins should hit it off real well."

Johnny felt like he had to help keep all these names and faces straight, since it was his house. It helped that Billy and the twins had red hair, too — easy to keep them in a group.

"So, Rebecca and Sissy belong to Aunt Victoria and Uncle Robert. That's easy to remember — they all have blond hair."

"Yeah!" Silas was getting into the game now. "And we can remember Martha and William go together because "M" for Martha is just "W" for William upside down!"

The adults all laughed at the earnestness of the children. They were determined to get the names of all these people straight.

Lydia piped up, "And Billy is short for William, isn't it?"

Billy nodded and smiled shyly, pleased with the attention.

Lucy asked solemnly, holding Loreen's hand, "What about us? How will you remember us?"

Elizabeth, the only other five-year-old in the room, grabbed Lucy's hand and pulled her toward the stairs. "I'll remember you because we'll be havin' a tea party!" And they ran up the stairs.

Victoria looked at the remaining children in the house. "Why don't ya'll go on outside or upstairs or somewhere to play?"

After they all clomped up the stairs, she added, "And let us get some peace and quiet!"

"Yes, it is a houseful," admitted Ruth. "But, as Pa would have said, 'we wouldn't have it any other way!' " chorused the adults.

CHAPTER **17**

Train Travel

Without even trying, James had designed his house perfectly for a family reunion. There were five large bedrooms upstairs, plenty for guests, especially when the children give up their beds. There are extra feather mattresses to throw on the floor for anyone who has donated a bed or for guests who didn't call "Dibs!" quickly enough.

Downstairs included a kitchen area with plenty of room for chopping, kneading, rolling and stirring as well as a long wooden table with benches to seat eight on each side, more if some of them are children. The rest of downstairs had lots of room where they could be together. Plenty of comfortable chairs to draw up close to the fireplace, but not so big that sitting at the table excluded anyone from the conversation. It was a wonderful, cozy home.

Everyone settled into seats around the room. Martha told them about the trip from Atlanta. "I'd forgotten how cold it is up here!" she exclaimed, pulling her shawl tighter around her shoulders. "It's quite warm at Christmastime in Georgia."

She glanced at William who raised his eyebrows at her. "But I promised my husband I wouldn't complain about the cold if he let me come visit for the holidays."

Ruth put her arm around Martha's shoulder and told her, "And we are so happy you could come. It will be a real family celebration. Tell us more about your trip up here."

"We were on the train for eighteen hours from Atlanta to Charlotte. That's where we met up with Vic and Robert. We stayed that night in a boarding house — the children were running around and we were playing cards and completely annoying all the other guests," said Martha.

Victoria added, "It took us about ten hours on the train to Charlotte. When I think about it, I can't quite believe we actually met up with them at the station because no schedules are written down." Then she proudly told her story of how the station master complimented her on her idea of little timetables.

Martha continued, raising one eyebrow at her sister, "Anyway, the next day we got up early and went to the station so we'd be sure not to miss the train up here. Like Vic said, though, no one knows when it's actually going to come so you just have to get there and wait. It's so frustrating."

"Then when it finally came we were on it for . . . guess how long!" Victoria demanded.

"Ten hours?"

"Fourteen?"

"Seventy-eleven?" guessed three-year-old Abigail, who preferred the comfort of her mother's lap to playing with all those children.

"Well, that's close," laughed Victoria. "Actually, we were on that silly train for thirty-six more hours. I didn't think we'd EVER get here."

"It was a beautiful train, though, and it wasn't a terrible trip," conceded Martha.

Martha and Victoria looked at each other and at the

same time said, "Now that we're off of it!" Everyone laughed and Martha groaned, "Oh no! I'm already worried about the trip home again!"

Martha looked at her Hadley relatives and asked, "Have you been on a train trip like that before?"

Ruth and Hanna shook their heads.

"What are the cars like?" asked Hanna.

Martha pursed her lips and said, "Actually, except for the time involved, it's all very comfortable."

"If you know where to sit," laughed William. "We didn't figure it out right away. We're lucky the train wasn't too crowded. You see, there's an aisle up the middle of the seats, which are very comfortable, by the way. They're plush red velvet armchair benches that seat two adults, or one of us and a bunch of kids. I counted that each car can seat about fifty-eight people. Well, about halfway back and off to one side is the wood stove that heats the car. We were cold when we first got on so we sat close to the stove. But after a little while, it got too hot so we moved all the way back from it. Then we froze! Finally, we found just the right spot . . . but it took a while."

Victoria continued, "Like William said, though, it was comfortable enough. You can change the backs of the seats around if you want to face the other direction. And there was a toilet and a water tank . . . luckily! It was a little bit difficult to sleep. Not for the children — or William and Robert — they just sprawled out wherever and whenever they felt like it. But for Martha and me . . . well, it's just different for women."

"I wish they would sell food on the train. Every time there was a short stop and a place to buy food nearby, I'd send William and then worry until he was sitting next to me again. I don't know what he'd do if he got stuck in one of those tiny little towns." Martha fretted.

Ruth and Hanna exchanged glances.

"Oh, I didn't mean tiny little towns are bad. I just meant . . . oh, you know what I meant."

"Yes, we know, Miss Forgot-Her-Roots! You just remember YOU came from a tiny little town and they are just fine," teased Ruth.

"We had a little excitement on our trip," said Charles. "To light the cars at night they use candles . . ."

"They used oil lamps with glass chimneys on some," interrupted Victoria.

"Yes, I believe both are quite common. But once when our train lurched around a corner too fast, the flame started a small fire on the wall. Those cars are made out of wood, you know," Charles explained.

The women gasped.

"Oh, we got it right out, it was no problem," Charles said hurriedly. "More often, the problem is at the station. Those stations burn down all the time. I saw some that had been built of stone. I guess they learned the hard way. The sparks from the trains going by caught everything on fire."

"It happens around here, too," explained Sam. "The farmers who have the misfortune of living near the rail lines have sparks catch their fields and farm buildings on fire too often."

"Yes, and there are many other potential problems with train travel. I was chatting with the conductor and he told me some scary tales about trips he's been on. Once, he almost ran right off a drawbridge that was raised. There are no signals of any kind on these tracks, they have to pay close attention. And one time where two different rail lines crossed, he just barely missed a train coming on the other line. He said if he would have stuck his head out the window, his nose would have been shaved right off his face," said Thomas.

"Well, my biggest complaint is how long it all takes," remarked Martha. "We stopped at every little town and some places where you couldn't even *see* a town. We stopped whenever the conductor felt like stopping and we also had to stop about every two hours so they could forage for wood to stoke all the fires. And you know what," Martha was indignant. "I don't think they paid anyone for the wood they took."

Victoria said, "I'm just glad we're finally here in the frigid north country and can stay for a while."

CHAPTER 18

You Don't Know Slaves Like I Do

William turned to James sitting next to him. "Speaking of being up north . . . I didn't see anyone working the fields after we got up in your neck of the woods."

James knew exactly what William meant but he vowed to himself that he wasn't going to begin *this* conversation. He knew that William meant he didn't see any *slaves* working up here. Both William and Robert inherited a lot of money from their families and both owned slaves to do the work on their estates. James liked both of his brothers-in-law but couldn't understand their position on slavery. What's more, James knew if they began to talk about it, he might say something he ought not say.

Last week, he promised Ruth that he'd try to steer clear of the topic. He had told her, "I won't start anything, but if Will or Robert insists on discussing it, I will tell them what I think — even if it hurts my sisters' feelings. A man sometimes has to stand up for what he knows to be right."

It was part of what Ruth loved about James; he knew

his mind and had a clear conscience. She knew he wouldn't start any trouble, but she wasn't so sure about Robert or William. Sometimes she felt they tried to stir up trouble even if there wasn't any. It seemed they thought because they were rich, their opinions held more weight.

Glancing at Ruth, James tried to get out of answering with a joke. "If you hadn't noticed, it's about a hundred degrees below zero out there. No one can work in weather like that!"

Ruth tried to change the subject by saying, "That's a beautiful shawl, Vic . . ." But William interrupted. "You know, with slaves, it doesn't much matter what the weather is like. They have a job to do and they're expected to do it, regardless. If they can't or won't, they know they'll get the business end of the strap to remind 'em."

Robert nodded in agreement.

Samuel tried changing the subject, too. "Bet those kids are having fun up . . ."

William was determined to put forth his opinion on slavery, even though everyone in the house knew his views. "Without our slaves, the economy of this entire country would crumble. No one would make any money. If there were no slaves to do the work, I couldn't buy seed or a new team of horses or buy clothes for my family. That would mean the people I buy from wouldn't be able to buy anything from anyone, and they wouldn't be able to buy anything from anyone . . . and on it would go. That's what I mean about the economy crumbling. It's like ripples in a pond. And what in the world would the slaves do if we didn't take care of them?"

Ruth and Hanna exchanged glances, each knowing what was coming. This conversation seemed to occur every time they had any discussions with Southerners.

James could not bite his tongue any longer. "How about they could be free to work and live and go to school and raise families and go to church and not be afraid of white

— 90 —

people anymore? Maybe that's what they could do if you didn't . . . 'take care of them.' "

William and Robert both snorted with laughter while their wives looked like they wanted to crawl under their chairs with embarrassment.

"There are about four million slaves in the South right now. And don't tell me they would all be welcome to come up here, or to Baltimore with you, Charles, or to Philadelphia there with you, Tom. They'd take all the jobs away from whites up here and there'd be nothin' for any of you. They'd work for pennies a day and fill your streets with their ignorant ways . . ."

Hanna interrupted William. "They're only ignorant because you won't let them learn to read or write. You know as well as I do they can learn just like we do."

"I know nothing of the sort. And that is pretty noble talk from you. Not only are you a woman and can't possible understand the economics of this situation, but you also don't know slaves like I do."

Samuel had to look away or William would see his smile start to take shape. William didn't know what an enormous can of worms he just opened. Hanna's eyes narrowed and her voice got low. "I am a woman, it's true, and there are things I don't know. But it's not because I'm a woman." She paused for effect. "It's because our newspapers only get delivered once in awhile out here in the boondocks."

Everyone was relieved that Hanna let the argument go with a joke, because she could have talked William into a frenzy — one where he would have wished he'd never come to Hadley for Christmas.

Instead, she let William off with a warning saying, "You have your beliefs and I have mine. But you have no right to tell me I'm wrong simply because I'm a woman. If my facts are wrong, that's a different matter and you can whip me in a fair argument. But you better have YOUR facts right, too, if you aim to tangle with me."

William stared at her for a moment, glad Martha didn't speak her mind the same way. He had never heard a woman speak like that to a man. In the South, women knew their place, he thought. But here, well . . . he couldn't believe what he was hearing. Finally, he smiled and said, "Hanna, I apologize. I forgot the manners my mother taught me. I do not wish to tangle with you, but if I ever do, I will watch my backside lest you give me another kick in the pants."

The adults laughed, glad the tension was over. The children, hearing the commotion, came charging down the stairs. "What's so funny?!" they all asked.

"Nothin,' " said Frank. "Who's ready to go find the most excellent Christmas tree?"

CHAPTER 19

The Perfect Christmas Tree

E veryone wanted to be involved in finding the perfect Christmas tree so they began to bundle up against the chill air. The sun was on the downhill side of daylight and shadows were lengthening. The adults helped the little ones with mittens, scarves, coats and boots. Some of the adults needed help, too.

"Hey Abbey! Help me with my mittens," whined Frank.

The three-year-old ran over to him, proud that she had been chosen to help an adult. When she saw him, though, she giggled. He was trying to cram his five big fingers into her tiny little mitten.

"Oh, Uncle Frank! Those are **my** mittens, you silly goose."

"Who are you calling a silly goose?! I'll silly goose you!" With that, Frank began chasing little Abigail around the room and out the front door. Abbey was laughing and squealing the whole time.

"Come on already. Last one to the edge of the forest is a rotten egg," Frank yelled.

Taking up the challenge, the rest of the children surged out the front door and across the yard. Not to be outdone by their younger brother, Charles, Thomas, Sam and James looked at each other and took off like horses spooked by lightning.

Tosh realized something interesting and potentially fun was happening without her. She ran across the yard in the middle of everyone, moving left and right, dodging here and there, nudging this way and that. Sam noticed her and was impressed. Here was definitive proof that Tosh *was* an excellent herding dog — she was herding the family.

"Why aren't you racing?" Victoria teased Robert and William.

"Well, I don't see you avoiding rotten egg status either," Robert shot back.

Before the men knew what was happening, Victoria and Martha had grabbed the hems of their dresses and ran twenty yards ahead of them. Robert and William forgot that their wives had grown up here and raced their brothers all over these lands. They realized this race was probably over before it began, but they gamely took off after the women.

Hanna and Ruth were left walking behind the group. They linked arms to steady themselves over the rough terrain.

"My land! What a noisy bunch we have here!" exclaimed Ruth. They could hear the excited shouts of their family up ahead of them arguing the virtues of each potential Christmas tree. They walked quietly toward the group, savoring the beauty of the winter scene.

The stand of pungent fir trees ahead of them interrupted the rolling hills all around them. Snow covered the hills in various patchwork patterns, with some areas filled with glittery snow and others dry, depending on the whim of the sun. The trees in the orchard stood straight and still, like soldiers at attention.

Hanna finally spoke. "I declare I don't know what will happen if we do go to war. If it comes, then it will force brothers to fight against brothers. We already know how Will and Robert feel, livin' down South where they do."

"I really try to understand and empathize with what they say and believe . . . " Ruth struggled to put her thoughts into words. "But I just can't agree that making money is more important than people. And that seems to be where Will always ends up with his arguments. Does the entire South really believe that slaves need to do all the hard work so that rich men like Robert and Will can become even richer? I don't know. I just hope Mr. Lincoln can work it all out for us."

Hanna agreed, "Mr. Lincoln seems to be a good man, trying to do what's right. Let's hope everyone can compromise so it doesn't come to war. That's never any solution."

Frank had snuck around a tree then suddenly came up behind them and yelled, "What's with all the serious faces?"

Both women, jumping like cats under a rocking chair, started talking at once. "I declare, Frank! You are as obnoxious as you were when you were ten!"

"Just for that, you get none of my mincemeat pie for dessert tonight."

But they couldn't be angry for long as he gave them his very contrite, sad face. "I reckon that was a baaaaaad thing to do to the most beautiful, intelligent, funniest, adorable . . ."

"Oh stop that and show us the tree you picked out." They could hear the axe strokes echoing out of the forest.

"Only if I get some pie tonight," bargained Frank.

The men were taking turns with the axe to chop down the prettiest spruce tree in the forest. It was perfectly symmetrical and full on all sides.

"I reckon it's the best one in the forest," Johnny declared.

Silas wasn't so sure. He liked the taller, skinnier one farther in. "Next year I'm comin' back for that one, even if I have to chop it down by myself," he vowed.

The men had shed their coats and worked up both a sweat and an appetite. Finally, someone yelled, "There she goes!" and the tree crashed on to the forest floor.

They gathered up the axes, put on their coats and mittens again, and everyone tried to grab a section of tree to help carry it. The twins, Lucy and Loreen, couldn't find a good place to scoot in and help. Charles called them over, saying, "Come here, girls. We can't lift it without you."

As they positioned themselves and started to grab hold, Charles winked at Thomas and everyone else lifted the fat little tree. The girls assumed they were responsible for lifting it.

Loreen said knowingly, "Uncle Charles, it's a good thing we came along. Otherwise we'd have to decorate our tree out here!"

They returned to the house at a much slower pace than they had run to the forest, and set the tree in a bucket of water when they finally got there.

"Nothing to eat till ya'll get the sap off your hands," warned Ruth.

Chapter 20

Talkin' By The Fire

After eating dinner and cleaning up afterward, everyone felt drowsy and content to sit by the fire and talk. The children had decorated the tree with the ornaments they had made. When they had strung something onto every visible branch, they admired their handiwork and settled in with the adults.

"Ya'll did a wonderful job with that old tree," commented Martha.

"It looks like livin' here in this house agrees with it," Frank said approvingly. "We don't get Christmas trees in Texas. But one year we stuck beans on the prickles of all the cactuses as far as we could see."

"You did not," exclaimed Mary. "That isn't Christmas-y at all!"

Frank protested. "Well, we did too. It was all we had. But you didn't want to be around those trees when they all started passin' gas."

The children and men howled with laughter while the

women looked at Frank with that disapproving "I-can't-believe-you-just-said-that" look.

The big table where they all ate dinner was pushed against the wall and out of the way. All the chairs in the house were brought into the main room, but there still weren't enough. Frank, Thomas and the children sat on the wood floor.

Frank turned to his brother and said, "Tom, I'm used to sittin' on the floor, but I'm young and handsome. What're you doin' down here?"

"Frank, my boy, I don't know about you bein' all that handsome or even very young, but I am hopin' you're goin' to be able to help me up when I need to go to bed tonight," joked Thomas.

Everyone sat in a big group, comfortable in front of the blazing fire. The children found space on the floor to lean against someone's chair, or play with their dolls, or enjoy a game of checkers. It was calm and quiet.

"You think they'll do it this year?" asked Uncle Frank to no one in particular.

"Who'll do what?" asked Ruth.

"Well, the animals, of course," Frank said, shaking his head.

"What are you talkin' about, Uncle Frank? What will the animals do?" asked little Abbey.

Frank looked at his brother Sam. "I can't believe you never told your children about the magic that happens in the barn on Christmas Eve."

All the children began talking at once. "Magic! Oh boy! What kind of magic? What do they do?"

"Hush up a minute and I'll tell you. Golly, you're a noisy bunch." Frank waited until he had their attention.

"On only one night, Christmas Eve, all the barnyard animals in the world can talk."

The children's eyes grew wide with amazement, while

Johnny and Silas exchanged a knowing look. The youngest children looked to their parents for confirmation. Seeing the nods and smiles, they turned back to Uncle Frank to go on.

"Remember that baby Jesus was born in a stable? Well, the animals that were there took such good care of him and his parents that God granted all animals this gift as a reward." Frank paused and looked at Tosh curled in a ball near the fire. "Well, not all animals, just the ones who live in barns. What do you think they talk about?"

Elizabeth, the deep thinker, said, "They probably talk over their plans for the year. You know, who will be the barnyard leader, who is responsible for babies whose mothers can't take care of them, if they're going to let Tosh tell them what to do again this year. That sort of thing."

"Why, Elizabeth, you are a true philosopher. What do you think they talk about, Lydia?" Frank asked.

Eight-year-old Lydia thought for a moment. "I think they probably ask each other questions they've been wondering about all year. The sheep would ask each other things like 'Why do you always get to eat first? How 'bout lettin' me have first crack at dinner once in awhile?' and they'd ask the rooster 'Why do you insist on waking us up so early?' You know, things like that," she said knowingly.

"I'd like to ask the rooster that myself!" agreed James.

"Except we all know that if there are any people around, the magic doesn't work," interjected Frank.

Mary had been quiet through the entire discussion. Finally, she turned to her mother and asked, "Is that true?"

Ruth looked at Mary's expectant face and chose her words carefully. "Sometimes we have to believe in things we may not understand. Especially if it's something we want to believe and if believing in it doesn't hurt anyone. But you can't force someone to believe what they don't want to."

Everyone pondered Ruth's words while they sat and listened to the crackling fire.

Breaking the silence after several minutes, Robert winked at Hanna and said, "You know, I don't want to get into the slavery issue with Will and Hanna again, but the news I hear looks like we'll need more than Christmas magic to solve these disagreements."

"These disagreements" everyone knew to be the two issues dividing the country — slavery and a concept called "States' Rights."

Robert continued, "Just before we left South Carolina, our legislature voted to secede from the Union. We don't want to be a part of the union of states any longer."

The group gasped. This was more serious than they had thought.

"Yes, we're none too happy with that Lincoln there in Washington," added William. "When he won the presidency this year by saying he'd end slavery . . ."

Thomas interrupted, "Lincoln didn't say he'd abolish slavery. He only said he wouldn't tolerate expanding slavery into any new territories. But you in the South won't compromise with him and now it's looking like this is only going to get worse."

"Well, Tom, we just can't abide Lincoln's views." William predicted, "I won't be surprised if our men in Georgia decide to secede, too. You see, we in the South don't manufacture very many products. Mostly we send our raw materials like cotton up north to places like Baltimore so people like Charles can turn our cotton into cloth. Then they send the cloth, or even the finished shirts and dresses, back down to us. But our taxes are outrageously high. Many Southerners feel we can do without our dependency on your manufactured products."

The women had stricken looks on their faces.

Robert tried to console them. "Now, don't you women start frettin' over this. The North is not going to fight a war with the South over things like secession and slavery. It will work itself out soon enough."

Everyone in the room hoped what he said was true, but not one of them truly believed it.

CHAPTER 21

Christmas Morning, 1860

Finally, the day the children had been waiting for —
Christmas morning at last. The tree looked beautiful with
the morning light shining on it from the window. There were
piles of gifts under the tree wrapped in pretty paper and tied
with colorful ribbon. There were also twelve oranges and
twelve little red packages under the tree, one for each child.

Johnny looked at his sister Lydia. "That paper isn't
like any of the other paper we have," he said quietly, pointing
at the twelve small packages.

Lydia studied them on her hands and knees. "You're
right — where'd they come from?" she questioned.

Frank overheard their conversation. "It's a puzzler,
indeed," he agreed.

"Do you think it could be from Santa?" Lydia asked
incredulously.

"I reckon you've been good enough for Santa to visit.
Maybe so," agreed Frank, walking away from them with a
twinkle in his eye.

Everyone who had been staying at Samuel's house rode up in the wagon just as breakfast was ready.

"Whooee! Get me some coffee in these frozen hands!" hollered Samuel.

Without taking her eyes off the bread she was slicing, Ruth said, "I believe you've been here enough to know where the stove is. And I reckon you can figure out how to pour it into a cup, too, unless you're royalty all of a sudden."

Everyone laughed as Sam blushed and looked a little sheepish. He went to the stove and carried the coffee pot over to where Ruth stood, still slicing bread.

Giving a deep elaborate bow from the waist, he said in his silliest regal voice, "Now M'Lady, would you be takin' cream from the royal cow in your royal coffee?"

Ruth gave a deep curtsy, responding in her silliest regal voice, "Yes, Your Highness, please to give me a royal lump of sugar, too."

Rolling her eyes, Hanna said, "I'll give you both a royal lump if you don't give me that coffee pot. Some of us are freezin' to death here."

Johnny piped up and declared, "Yes, and some of us royal princes and princesses are starvin' to death, too!"

"Ooh, am I a princess?" asked Abigail, clapping her hands.

"Yes, you are," cooed Sam, her father, "and we'll get you some breakfast right now."

The women started moving platters of food from the kitchen to the table. The table groaned with the weight of steaming bowls of scrambled eggs, bacon, sausage, grits and porridge, as well as cold pitchers of milk, various jams and jellies, and three different kinds of coffee cakes.

The children lined up first with their plates in their hands. The older children helped the younger kids fill their plates. They then carefully carried them to any open place on the floor they could find.

"Honestly, it's a good thing I swept the floor again this morning. It's getting good use as a table," commented Ruth.

The men stayed out of the way drinking coffee and talking in low voices until it was their turn to line up for breakfast. The adults found room to eat sitting on the chairs in front of the fireplace. Then, when each person was full as a tick, they all pitched in to clean up.

After the kitchen resembled more of a kitchen again and less of a disaster area, they all went out to where the beautiful Christmas tree waited and began to exchange their gifts. The men admired the scarves the women knitted for them and the women admired the aprons with all the delicate stitchery on them. Sam and James surprised the women by giving them each a carved wooden footstool they had made in their spare time. At his blacksmith shop, Thomas had forged each family a bootscraper to place by their doors.

Charles had not seen the gift his wife picked out for him to give to his brothers and sisters before that moment. Each family opened a package containing a tea cozy decorated with crabs, seashells and an embroidered "Greetings from Baltimore!" Charles was more than a little embarrassed. He knew his brothers and sisters wouldn't have any idea what a tea cozy was. But after studying the two half circles of fabric sewn together with the straight part at the bottom left open and seeing Charles' face, they began to guess what this gift could be.

"Look! It's a hat!"

"No, it's to carry muffins in!"

"No, it's a foot warmer for my bed!"

"No, it's . . . it's a . . . . Hey, Charles, what the heck is it anyway?!"

Charles had to laugh. They were so earnest in their guessing, but so wrong. "Well, I guess out here in the boon-docks you're not as sophisticated as we are in Baltimore. This here," he explained, picking up Ruth's tea cozy, "is to keep your teapot warm. After you brew your tea, you put this here coat on it so it stays warm until you can drink it all."

The group thought about that explanation for a minute, looked at each other and laughed uproariously. Charles looked at them with one eyebrow cocked, waiting for them to finish. Finally, Hanna said, "Charles, please thank Annie for this gift and don't you dare tell her any of this. But really, when have you ever seen us drinking a cup of tea? We keep the coffee pot on the stove all day, remember?"

"Now Hanna, don't you remember last week when the Queen of England came over? We could have really used this then," Ruth teased, winking at Charles.

That set off another round of laughter. Charles pretended he was getting annoyed, but he knew they were right. Having grown up in Baltimore, his wife had no idea about life in the country. Finally, sweet little Elizabeth said, "Uncle Charles, I think it's beautiful. Can I have it for my tea set?"

"Of course you can, you adorable child you. You're the only one who deserves to have a wonderful tea cozy like this anyway." With a flourish, Charles presented one of them to Elizabeth and then stuck his tongue out at his brothers and sisters.

When the gift giving resumed, Martha and Victoria surprised them all by giving each person storebought clothes — dresses for the women and girls, shirts for the men and boys.

"Victoria, Martha, this is too much. You must have spent a fortune on these. They're beautiful!" Everyone was talking at once. Then all the women jumped up and ran upstairs to put on their new dresses. Clothing from a store was very extravagant and very special.

"I haven't seen so much excitement since Ruth won first place for her crabapple jelly at the county fair. And she only won a blue ribbon then. Are you sure this didn't cost too much?" asked James warily.

"Don't you worry about what we do with our money," scolded Martha.

"Yes," added Robert. "We have plenty and there's no reason we can't share a little of our southern hospitality with you."

Charles and Thomas exchanged an uneasy glance. They weren't sure why, but they felt this was more than a nice Christmas gift. Maybe it was to show that the South had better things than they did in the North. Maybe it was showing off their money. Or maybe it was just a friendly gift for Christmas.

No one said anything more than "thank you."

When the women came down, everyone admired the fancy clothes. They wore them all day, even when they cooked. But they made the children change back into their everyday clothes and save these for church.

The children couldn't wait any longer to open up the pretty red packages. They tore into them and found twelve different little toys — jacks, spinning tops, carved wooden animals and some they weren't sure *how* to play with!

Rebecca looked around the room. "Who do we say thank you to?"

The adults looked at one another. "Well, I guess you need to thank Santa Claus," decided Thomas.

In unison, the children all yelled "Thank you, Santa" at the top of their lungs.

CHAPTER 22

North vs. South, Kid Version

For the next few days after Christmas, there was lots of eating and laughing and talking among the adults. They had quietly agreed to disagree about the slavery issue because there was no more talk about it. This topic was replaced with an understanding that they had their own opinions based on information formed from their own experiences.

So they concentrated on catching up with each others lives and remembering when they were kids. After this visit, who knew when they would see each other again?

The children played and played with their new toys from Santa. The Hadley cousins delighted in showing their southern cousins what country living was all about.

There had not been any more snow so they were able to run through the fields and forests, playing all kinds of games using only their imaginations. They even showed their city cousins how to do various chores around the farms. The favorite, by far, was trying to milk the cows. It was probably not the favorite for the cows, however.

"Hey c'mon!" Johnny called everyone and ran to the middle of the yard near the farmhouse. "You're leaving today so this is your last chance for swingin'!"

He climbed up the rope attached to the huge tree in the yard and let loose a great yell while swinging from it. Johnny was trying to show his cousins how he could hold the rope and turn upside down while swinging. He couldn't remember a time when the great sycamore tree didn't have a long rope hanging from its sturdiest branch. It just occurred to him that his father would have had to shimmy up the trunk to tie the rope on. The image made him laugh so hard, his arms got weak and he dropped to the ground.

"What's the matter? You used to could do that, no problem!" Silas questioned.

" 'Used to could do that' — what does *that* mean?" demanded Rebecca. "I've never heard anyone in South Carolina say *that*." Rebecca was ten and knew it all.

"What do you mean 'what does it mean'? It means exactly what I said!" Silas wasn't used to being questioned by anyone, especially a girl. He didn't much like it.

"In the South we have something you'll never have up here," said nine-year-old Sissy.

"Yeah," interrupted Johnny. "Bossy girls!"

Johnny and Silas laughed. Their sisters didn't know whose side to take in this argument. Should they be true to their siblings or to their gender?

"No," continued Sissy. "You'll never have manners, genteel manners. It's what makes a true lady and a true gentleman. It's obvious by the way you talk."

Silas didn't quite know what to say. His manners had never been called into question before, aside from his parents telling him to chew with his mouth closed or close the door when he came in. How many times had he heard "are you being raised in a barn?" from his parents.

Johnny, too, felt he needed to vindicate himself. "Well, Smarty Pants. I'll tell you one thing we're happy we *don't* have that you have in the South."

They eyed each other like two porcupines on a narrow path.

"Slaves!" he yelled. "You really think you're sumthin' special just because you have slaves do all your work for you. But you're not. You aren't even nice to them and when President Lincoln frees them, like my daddy says he will, then you'll be poor, too, and you'll have to do all your own work." Johnny's face matched his red hair he was so angry.

Rebecca and Sissy were horrified. No one can talk to them that way and compare them to a slave doing slave's work. They could think of nothing to say to their cousins, though, so they stomped back to the house, slamming the door behind them.

"Uh oh, Johnny," Silas said. "Now you've done it."

Johnny began to get nervous about what his mother would do when she learned he got into a fight with his cousin, his girl cousin no less.

"Well, I don't care what she says. Just because they have lots of money doesn't mean they can go around owning people and telling me I don't talk right! I hope there IS a war and they lose." With that, Johnny climbed up into the hayloft in the barn and sat down.

It wasn't nearly as much fun to play without Johnny and Silas so the rest of the children climbed up, too. The younger kids didn't understand what the argument was about, just that there was an argument. But the older ones, Lydia and Mary, and Billy from Atlanta, did understand.

Billy's family owned slaves also, but he was silent throughout the entire exchange between his cousins.

"You know," Billy started slowly. "I've been thinkin' about it. If there is a war, no one's really going to win anything. My daddy says that without slaves you won't get any cotton to make cloth up here. So factories like Uncle Charles' won't make any money and no one will have any jobs and it will just go around like that all the time and get worse and worse."

Billy was out of breath when he finished. He was only seven, but really had thought about it a lot. Still, he didn't want to offend his cousins whom he had come to like on this visit to the north. He also remembered what happened to Rebecca and Sissy, and preferred to stay on Johnny's good side.

The long silence worried Billy. Were they mad at him for what he said? He made sure he didn't make fun of the way they talked or the things they said. Finally, Lydia spoke. She too had remained silent during the argument between her brother and her cousin. "I think he's right," she said, referring to Billy. "If there is a war, it isn't going to matter what they're fighting about. People will still die or get hurt and everyone will be sad."

The children thought about that for a while and came to the conclusion that none of them wanted war.

"But we don't need to worry," decided Silas. "Because none of us will go off to war. There's enough work to do on our farms and we're too young, anyway."

They all felt a little better about the entire situation. Johnny had even forgotten he was worried about his mother getting angry at him for arguing with his cousins. Until he saw her come out the door, that is.

"Everybody down here!" she called to them. "It's time to say our good-byes!"

Johnny couldn't believe his ears. Rebecca and Sissy hadn't ratted on him! Now he didn't quite know what to think about them. They seemed like tattle-tails.

Everyone climbed down the ladder and had one last swing before all the relatives left to go back to their own homes. They all agreed it was a great Christmas reunion.

CHAPTER 23

Secession — February, 1861

Hey, Ma! Pa!" Silas shouted excitedly. He searched through the crowd outside Hawkin's store until he saw his father's weathered hat above the crowd. Next to his father, he saw his mother holding Abigail, waiting patiently for their turn to talk to the blacksmith. The visit from the relatives had been lots of fun and quite a diversion, but now their lives were back to normal.

Silas pushed his way through the knot of people with his sister Elizabeth right behind him. He reached his parents in time to hear his father say, "I guess all this cold weather is good for business, eh, Hiram?"

"Indeed it is, Sam," replied the smithy rather sheepishly. "But I don't take kindly to profiting from another's misfortune. I hope no one sees it that way."

Sam and Hanna both laughed. "Of course not, Hiram," Hanna said kindly. "You have to make a living too. It's not your fault farm machinery cracks when it gets too cold for too long."

"Is it?" teased Sam. "You don't come sneakin' around in the night, do you, Hiram? Breakin' our machines?"

Flustered, Hiram looked up from the metal he was soldering. When he saw the twinkle in Sam's eye, he laughed. "Any more of that and you'll have to fix your own problems, Mr. Jackman," he said, trying to be stern, but instead he just made everyone laugh.

Silas tugged on his father's sleeve. "Pa, look at this," he insisted.

Silas handed the newspaper to his father. Hanna leaned over to look, too.

"Well, lookee there," said Sam, pointing to an article. "Anderson's cow got stuck in a ravine last week and it took eight men to get her out."

"No, Pa, this one," Silas said impatiently.

The crowd quieted when Sam began to read out loud.

"On January 26, the year of our Lord 1861, several states showed their contempt for the United States of America by voting to secede from the Union."

Five-year-old Elizabeth interrupted. "What does "secede" mean?"

Her mother answered her. "It means they don't want to be part of the United States anymore. They're going to leave the Union."

"Who, Sam? Read the rest!" the small crowd urged.

Sam continued, "It says, let's see, where was I . . . Mississippi, Florida, Alabama, Georgia and Louisiana."

The crowd was silent, each person thinking his or her own thoughts. The only sound was the hiss and crackle from the blacksmith's fire. Sam broke the silence, declaring, "Well, gentlemen, it appears there will indeed be a war in our future."

Hiram turned back to his work and the crowd began to leave the blacksmith's shop. They didn't know exactly how, but everyone knew their lives would never be the same.

CHAPTER 24

Hawkins General Store

About a month later, Johnny had been to town to pick up some thread for his mother at Hawkin's store. He loved everything about the general store and was always happy to do his mother the favor of going there.

He loved the big covered porch with the benches where the townsfolk sat in the summer and gossiped about this and that. He loved to read the news that was posted in front of the store — the baby born, the barnraising party for the family whose barn had burned down, the team of horses for sale. Because there was no local newspaper for Hadley, this was what they had instead.

Johnny stopped to admire the display of clothes in the two large windows on either side of the door. Men's clothing on the left, women's on the right. He giggled at the thought of his father wearing the fancy clothing with the top hat modeled by the mannequin. He knew his father would feel more at home with the overalls and boots displayed next to the mannequin.

His mother, however, would love the fancy dresses displayed in the other window. But he could hear her now saying, "I don't need anything that fancy to do my chores . . . although it would be nice for wearing to church . . . That cotton fabric inside is good enough . . . I don't need someone else making clothes for me . . . that's just too extravagant." Then she'd take one last look at the dresses in the window, sigh, and walk into the store to buy more practical things.

Johnny also loved opening the squeaky screen door and being overwhelmed by the assault of odors that hit him all at once — leather, coffee, spices, cotton fabric, jams and jellies, apples, sweets, perfumes. As he walked in the store and let the door bang shut behind him, he closed his eyes and tried to guess which smells he was smelling. It was a game he rarely won.

This time, as he walked in, he was alone except for the two old-timers playing checkers in the corner by the potbellied stove. Even though it was Saturday, the busiest day for the general store, Johnny had arrived early, before the crowd.

Johnny could hear Mr. Hawkins in the back room moving things around, probably getting ready for all the customers to arrive.

Johnny didn't mind waiting at all, though. In fact, he loved looking at all the items in the store — everything from common goods they used at his house to extravagant items they could never afford. There was a dollhouse high on a shelf, away from little fingers, that Lydia and Mary have stared at for many hours, playing with it in their imaginations.

Over in the opposite corner from the checker game was the post office. Abel Hawkins was also the postmaster. There were cubby holes labeled A to Z where he would sort the mail that came whenever the train stopped in Hadley. Johnny saw nothing in the "J" cubby so he knew there was no mail for the Jackman family.

He moved to his right to look at the display of tools.

There were tools for all sorts of jobs, many of which he couldn't even guess their use.

His eyes moved up and down the shelves that reached to the ceiling. Hawkins puts the more expensive items like perfume and pens and the breakable items like dishes and medicine bottles high up to keep them out of danger. On the lower shelves, he puts the more commonly needed, and less breakable, items like pots and pans, fabric bolts and wooden items.

Along the sides of the store in front of these shelves ran two long counters. Mr. Hawkins and his wife would stand behind them to wait on the customers. Built into the counters were the drawers and bins that held the coffee, spices, flour, sugar and other items people bought in bulk.

Most people brought their own burlap or cloth bags to hold what they wanted to purchase, then Hawkins would weigh them. The farmers who lived way out of town always tried to buy enough to last them a good long time. They didn't want to make the trip into town very often.

Most customers would barter their goods with Hawkins. They'd load up their wagons with homemade bread, jellies, produce grown on their farms, eggs and anything else they thought Hawkins would take in trade for his goods in the store. Mr. and Mrs. Hawkins worked long hours in the store so they were happy to trade for things that they didn't have time to make for themselves. Abel especially liked it when women brought in homemade pies to trade for his fabric or household items they needed.

Almost everyone dealt with credit at the general store. They'd bring in whatever they had to barter and Mr. Hawkins would come up with a fair price for it. Then he'd write this amount in his ledger. Every time they came in to buy something, he'd reduce their credit by that amount.

Sometimes the farmers used up all their credit before their next harvest, but Hawkins knew he dealt with a trustworthy bunch of folks and never thought twice about extending credit even when there was nothing to barter. Hawkins knew he'd be paid as soon as it could be managed. It was a good arrangement for everyone.

Abel Hawkins went to Philadelphia once every year to buy more goods for his store. He always let people know well in advance of his trip so they could tell him of any special orders they wanted him to pick up while he was there. People always wanted him to buy special books, or a fancy hat, or a pocket watch — things he didn't normally carry in his store.

As Johnny's eyes moved around the room, they spied the big glass jars of candy on the counters. So much candy! And so many different kinds! Each one seemed better than the last.

Mr. Hawkins jarred him out of his candy reverie. "Well, hello there, Johnny. I hope you haven't been waiting out here too long. You should have called me out from the storeroom."

"Nah, it's all right, Mr. Hawkins. I was just lookin' around. I need some white thread for my mother. Oh, and something else . . . what was it . . ."

Oh, yes, now he remembered. When his father heard he was going to town, he asked him to buy a newspaper also.

"And a newspaper, if you have one."

"I do indeed have one newspaper left. Been savin' it for your pa, too. I know how he likes to read the paper while he soaks in the tub." With a wink, he reached down behind the counter for the newspaper.

Abel Hawkins was the only man in town to subscribe to a newspaper. He had a friend at the newspaper office in Staunton who sent along a few extra copies of the paper. He sold them to the townsfolk who were interested in current events and who could read.

Hawkins was right — there was nothing James liked

better than reading the paper while he took his Saturday evening bath. Although in March that can be cold!

As Johnny was leaving the store, Mr. Hawkins tossed him a lollipop.

"Gee, thanks, Mr. Hawkins!"

CHAPTER 25

We Must Not Be Enemies

When Johnny got home, his mother had a tall glass of ice cold milk and a thickly sliced piece of bread hot from the oven waiting for him. As she spread butter on the bread, Johnny put the thread and the newspaper down on the table. He watched the butter melt and disappear into the aromatic bread. The room smelled like warm yeast.

"How'd you know I was starvin'?" Johnny asked his mother.

"You're always starvin,' that's how," his mother teased, patting his cheek. "Hey! This is white thread. I told you to get black. Get back to town. Come on, hurry up!"

Johnny was just ready for his first bite of the buttery goodness of his mother's bread. He stopped the bread just in front of his mouth and looked at his mother. Another five miles walk into town? He inwardly groaned, racking his brain to remember if she asked him for white or black thread.

"Kidding! Eat your food," she laughed. Johnny should know his mother by now. She just loved to tease him. "It was silly of me to run out of thread for these dresses I'm making for the girls. After all, I've never been able to sew without thread! Thank you for goin' to town for me. If I had to go, I don't know how I would have finished all these chores." She picked up the newspaper to move it out of her way. As she was putting it down, something caught her eye.

"Look Johnny. It's President Lincoln's speech from his Inauguration," she showed him the article. "Go get your father."

"What's an inauguration?" asked Johnny, thinking it was more war news.

"It's the ceremony in which they make someone the President of the United States," she answered. "It was on March 4th."

James, Ruth and their children sat around the kitchen table. Ruth had scanned the article while Johnny was gathering everyone. She said, "Lincoln says he has no intention of abolishing slavery where it is already, and he is very much against any state seceding from the Union."

Lydia said, "That's just what Uncle Thomas said at Christmastime. He's smart."

"Yes, he is," agreed Ruth. "Listen to this. *My country-men, one and all, think calmly and well upon this whole subject. Nothing valuable can be lost by taking time. If there be an object to hurry any of you in hot haste to a step which you would never take deliberately, that object will be frustrated by taking time; but no good object can be frustrated by it.*"

Johnny and Lydia looked quizzically at each other. "What in the world does that mean?" Lydia asked.

James answered them. "He's just saying to think before you do anything. Nothing can be gained by people going off and doing stupid things in the heat of the moment. Remember at Christmastime when we'd get into those arguments about slavery and such? We didn't always think before we spoke and rarely took into account the other person's feelings."

The children nodded, remembering.

"What else does he say, Ruth?"

"Well, let's see. *In your hands, my dissatisfied fellow countrymen, and not in mine, is the momentous issue of civil war. The government will not assail you. You can have no conflict without being yourselves the aggressors. You have no oath registered in Heaven to destroy the Government, while I shall have the most solemn one to preserve, protect and defend it.* I guess he's saying that he doesn't want to start war but he has a duty to continue the government as it is," Ruth continued. "There's more. *I am loath to close. We are not enemies, but friends. We must not be enemies. Though passion may have strained, it must not break, our bonds of affection. The mystic chords of memory, stretching from every battlefield and patriot grave to every living heart and hearthstone all over this broad land, will yet swell the chorus of the Union, when again touched, as surely they will be, by the better angels of our nature.*"

Everyone was quiet, studying what they had heard.

Johnny finally spoke. "Is he saying that because Americans have already been through so much together, and we know how bad war is, and that even though people from the North and the South think differently than each other, if we wait and think about what a war between the states would do to us all, then we won't do it?"

"Yes, I guess that about sums it up, son," replied James. "And not just our country, but our families, too. A war like this can tear apart families just as it can tear apart a country."

After sitting in silence for a few more minutes, James got up and walked slowly out of the room, carrying the newspaper with him. Ruth watched him go, wondering what he was thinking, but deep down not wanting to know.

CHAPTER **26**

War Declared — April, 1861

Another day brought another newspaper. This time
Samuel and James had been to town on this crisp clear
April day.

"Ruth!" James called. "I'm home!"

Ruth hurried out, drying her hands on her apron. "I
expected you back an hour ago. Where have . . ." She stopped
talking when she saw that Sam was with him. Both looked
grim. "What happened, what's the matter?" she demanded.

Sam handed her the newspaper. "War Declared" the
headline screamed.

The article in the newspaper explained that South
Carolina wanted the federal government to give up Fort
Sumter in Charleston. But ever since Lincoln took office, he
wanted to settle the matter without force. He finally decided
only to send food to Fort Sumter in unarmed ships, forcing
the South to take the next step. If they fired on an unarmed
ship that was peacefully bringing food to the fort, then
Lincoln would have no choice but to fight back. The South

began shelling the fort on April 12, 1861 and continued to do so for thirty-four hours. No one died, but the war had begun.

Ruth sunk into the nearest chair, her hand fluttered up to her face. "Oh, no," was all she managed to say.

Sam said simply, "I must go tell Hanna."

After Sam left, Ruth and James sat at the kitchen table, both lost in thoughts about the war. It seemed in direct contrast to the wonderful aromas that surrounded them. Ruth had been baking sourdough bread and stewing a chicken with onions and celery and powerful spices.

Ruth didn't know what to do so she got up and continued to cook. It's easier to deal with the unknown when you're doing something familiar and comfortable, she thought to herself.

After her husband's long silence, Ruth became uncomfortable. "It's not like you to be so quiet about something like this. What are you thinking?" she inquired gently.

James just stared at her, a faraway look on his face. Without speaking, he pushed his chair away from the table and walked over to his wife. His strong arms enveloped her for a moment. He let her go and silently walked out the kitchen door.

Ruth was terrified. "What is he thinking?" she whispered to herself as she watched him go.

CHAPTER 27

I'm Goin' to Fight

Samuel walked in the kitchen door of his farmhouse hollering, "Hanna! Hanna! Where are you?"

"Quiet down, you old . . . I just got Abigail to lay down for awhile. With you making so much noise . . ." Hanna stopped scolding when she saw the look in her husband's eyes. "What is it?" she asked quietly.

"We're at war," he said simply. "And I aim to go fight."

Hanna just stared at him, not understanding what he meant.

"I'm goin' to fight," Sam repeated.

Hanna couldn't believe her ears. She dropped silently into the closest chair. "You can't! What will we do? What about the sheep?" She got a funny look on her face, as if she just realized the importance of what he had told her. "What . . . what . . . if something happens to you?" she asked quietly.

"Aw, nothin's going to happen to me! This won't last long. I'll be home in a few days. And remember? I'm your hero!"

The day they went on the picnic and he "saved" her from the raccoon seemed a lifetime ago. Hanna realized this matter was not really up for discussion; her husband had already made his decision.

"Well, if you want to go fight for Mr. Lincoln and his Union . . ."

Sam interrupted her. "I'm not fightin' for the Union," he said gently. "I'm fightin' for the South."

Hanna felt a stab of fear. This couldn't be good, she thought. We don't even live in the South. What could he be talking about? Her mind raced with too many questions. Finally, she could form only one. "Why?" she asked angrily.

"Oh, Hanna." Sam struggled to find the right words to explain how he felt. "It isn't about slavery, if that's what you're thinkin.' I don't think it's necessarily right for men to own other men, but that's the way it is and has been for a long time. If the South can't use slaves, imagine what will happen to the economy. None of us will be able to survive. As much as I disagreed with Robert and Will at Christmastime, I've thought about it a lot since then. I think they're right when they say this country needs the institution of slavery."

Hanna started to say something but Sam, knowing she was angry, cut her off.

"But that's not all this war is about. In fact, the states' rights issue is more important to me. It just doesn't seem right that the government in Washington can tell each state what they can and cannot do."

When Sam had finished his explanation, Hanna just looked at him. It was obvious he had made up his mind and nothing she could say would change it. Her mind whirred with different emotions until she landed on one — fear.

She was right to be afraid for her husband.

"No good can come from this," she said simply and sadly, then walked out of the room.

CHAPTER 28

Decisions

James sat down on the woodpile. They've had so many good times on this farm. He remembered the times long ago when he and his brothers and sisters chased around these hills. His eyes twinkled with remembrance. And there was the time his dog Old Blue ate the Christmas turkey his Ma was cooling on the table. He laughed out loud at the memory of that long ago holiday.

His face darkened at the memory of a more recent Christmas and the discussion they had about the prospects for war. At the time, he didn't really think it would happen. It was unthinkable to James that anyone would want to dissolve the Union of the United States, much less fight to dissolve it.

James knew what he wanted to do — what he had to do — but did not want to tell his wife. Should he make it lighthearted so as not to worry her? Should he be grave and serious as he told her?

Finally, it was decided for him when Ruth came out and sat next to him on the woodpile. "I've been watchin' you out here, you old man. You're carrying on a conversation with yourself in your head. I saw you laughin,' then you'd get serious, then you'd cock your head like you were listenin' to somebody else, then you'd look like you were answerin' them back. Have you worked it out yet?"

James laughed at his wife. "Yes, I have," he said and put his arm around her shoulder, hugging her close. "You're too smart for me, Ruthie. I've been sitting here trying to figure out how to tell you something when you've known all along what I need to tell you."

"When do you have to leave?" she asked quietly.

The smile left James' face as he answered her. "I expect I'll go right away. Well, as soon as I help Sam shear the sheep in a few weeks. Johnny can cut the orchard grass. It'll just take him longer. Maybe he can even get his lazy uncle Samuel to help him. But I'll be back in time to help with the apple picking in October. This war can't last that long."

They sat together, thinking their thoughts.

Suddenly James said, "Ruth, I've got to do what I think is right. The most important thing is the Union. We need the South and they need us. It's not right for states to secede. The South started shelling Fort Sumter for no reason. The newspaper said Lincoln was sending food to them in unarmed ships and the Confederates started firing on them. That shows there is no compromise possible."

Ruth realized how passionate her husband was about his decision.

"I understand what you're telling me, James," Ruth began, "but I am not happy about it. I . . . I . . . don't know what we'll do without you. What was it Mr. Lincoln said? *Nothing valuable can be lost by taking time.* Have you thought this through all the way? Is it really the right thing to do?" Ruth looked at James who nodded slowly. "Well, then, I don't know how to tell the children. We'll miss you."

"Aw, that's the only reason I'm goin' — so I can have

you tell me nice things!" James' joke was bittersweet. He felt the same way but didn't want to worry his wife. "Besides, you'll have Sam just down the road for anything you can't handle. And I'll be back in the eye of a wink. I mean, the wink of an eye."

Ruth laughed in spite of the seriousness of the situation. "Let's go gather up the children. But *you* have to tell them. I'll not have them thinkin' it was my idea!"

CHAPTER 29

Brother vs. Brother

Y ou're what?!" James exploded in rage at his brother. "You're goin' to fight with the South?! The Confederates? I never knew my brother was a traitor."

The look in James' eyes was pure hatred. James and Ruth had gone to Sam's farm to tell them James was going off to fight for the Union. Sam had news of his own.

The conversation was not going well for any of them. Ruth and Hanna tried to keep the men calm, but James and Samuel were both completely furious and out of control.

Ruth tried to help. "James, if Sam believes that the states should govern themselves . . ."

"Then he's just as stupid as he looks!" James' words were being controlled by his anger.

Hanna jumped into the fray. "I'll not have you talkin' like that to my husband, you old fool. He knows exactly what he's doin' and his reasons make more sense than your reasons for joinin' the Union!"

"Now just one cotton pickin' minute," demanded

Ruth. "James is doin' the only honorable thing here. If brave men don't fight to save the Union, what future does this country have against lunkheads like Sam here?"

"Lunkheads?! Well, I never. You get out of my house this minute. And don't come back until you can keep a civil tongue in your mouth!" Hanna's face was beet red as she turned sharply and stormed out of the room.

The vein in Ruth's neck was throbbing. She stood motionless for a moment, then stomped out the front door of the farmhouse. "Pigs will fly before I set foot back in this place," she thought to herself.

The boys, Johnny and Silas, peered out from the side of the house, watching Ruth storm away home. They looked at each other, trying to understand. Never had they heard any of the adults speak in such a way or act so angry with anyone. Ruth didn't even yell like that the time Mr. Haney's goats got loose and ate her garden.

James came out of Sam's house, saw the boys and realized by their expressions they had heard every word that had been said.

He looked at them for a long time before he spoke. "This has nothin' to do with you boys. Or your sisters. It's just a little disagreement between grown-ups. I've already made my peace with your father, Silas. It will all be forgotten in a few days. I'll be back here to help with the shearing next week. Now let's go home, Johnny."

As they walked away, Johnny looked back at Silas. He wished he felt as confident as his father did.

Chapter 30

Sheep Shearing

Shearing day dawned hot and dry. Sam felt a hard knot that had been in his stomach all week start to fade away.

Hanna watched as her husband ate an enormous breakfast. "What in the world has gotten into you? You're eating like you haven't had a bite in a week!" she teased.

Sam laughed his hearty laugh. "Well, I feel like that's true! I've been so worried about it raining on the sheep. You obviously have never tried to shear wet wool! But since it's been hot and dry for the last few days, we can actually get to the shearing. This kind of weather brings the lanolin up in the wool so the skin stays drier and makes the shearin' much easier," he explained. He paused a moment then stole a glance at his wife. "I just wonder if James will be here."

Hanna narrowed her gaze. "For your sake, I hope he does because I know it's a difficult job and you need the help. But I refuse to be out there with him after what happened and all the horrible things he said."

Sam ate in silence for a few minutes, then asked

mischievously, "You'll still make my lunch, won't you?"

As she walked by him, she hit him over the head with the kitchen towel she was using to dry her hands and declared, "You old fool."

"Love your fried chicken!" Sam told her, ducking as she walked by him again.

He always made her laugh, even when she was annoyed. "Oh, alright. But you only get it cold and leftover. And no pie!" she stated emphatically.

Silas walked in the kitchen and saw his parents teasing each other. He smiled and hoped that meant everything between them and Uncle James and Aunt Ruth will be okay now. The memory of his mother so angry still scared him.

As Silas and Sam were finishing up their breakfast, they heard the clomp-clomp-clomp of boots on the porch. James and Johnny stuck their heads in the door.

"Can we come in?"

Hanna set her jaw stubbornly and turned back to the stove.

Sam smiled with relief. "Yes, of course! Did you eat?"

"We ate until we were about ready to burst. I knew Hanna wouldn't want to feed me today since everyone was so mad at me." James paused and hung his head, feeling out the situation in the kitchen, trying to gauge Hanna's mood.

He kept his head down but turned his eyes up to look at her. When he saw she had turned around and her face had softened, he said, "But I reckon she'd love a dance!" James grabbed her around the waist and twirled her around the kitchen. Hanna tried to be angry with him, but couldn't.

"You're just like your fool brother!" she said, laughing. "Now all of you get out of here and get to work." Hanna started swatting at them with her towel as they ran out of the kitchen.

Sam called over his shoulder, "Do we still get lunch?"

They laughed as they heard her call out, "Are you still

an old fool?"

In preparation for shearing day, Sam had set up a temporary pen to hold a few of the sheep. Sam and James had done this many times before but this was the first year the boys were allowed to help. They were excited to be involved in the actual shearing, rather than just watching from the fence, like last year, doing the little jobs like getting the extra shears or bringing in the next sheep.

"Okay, men, we have fifty-three sheep to shear. Let's get busy!"

With that, the boys herded a few sheep into the holding pen. James selected his first one, an enormous two-hundred-pound ram. He grabbed the sheep by one curled horn and led him into the barn.

"C'mon, you overgrown billy goat. Let's show these boys how it's done," James said, wrestling the big animal into place.

James sat the ram in an undignified position with his tail on the ground, his back against James' legs and his feet sticking straight out in front. James gripped him with his legs and his left hand and began clipping the ram's stomach with his right.

In less than five minutes, as the boys watched, off came the wool, all in one piece. James spread the wool flat on the floor of the barn.

Sam looked at it approvingly. "Must be twenty pounds of wool on that one!"

The sheep just stood there, naked and embarrassed. James took him back out to the pasture.

"Keep an eye on the rams after they get sheared. When they're naked like that they don't recognize each other and they start to fight. That's why we'll put them in different parts of the pasture when we release them."

Johnny and Silas were laughing at the sight of the huge ram with no wool. It was difficult to imagine something looking that funny being a danger to anything!

"This is not a game, boys. This is serious work and it needs to be done right if we're to make our money this season and keep the sheep safe and healthy. Now, c'mon, there's lots of work to do," Sam looked sternly at the boys who immediately got serious.

They went to the holding pen and each selected a smaller ewe to shear.

Sam began to give them pointers to make the job easier. Silas interrupted, "Aw, Pa, we've watched you do this every year. We know how to do it!"

Johnny agreed, "Yeah, we're not babies!"

"Suit yourselves," Sam shrugged his shoulders and went to choose his next victim.

As the boys both struggled with their ewes, trying to get them into position to shear AND hold onto them AND hold the clippers, their fathers watched out of the corners of their eyes. They understood the boys' need to prove they could do the job themselves, but they wanted to make sure the job was done correctly and safely for both sheep and boy.

Sam and James had each finished their next two sheep while the boys continued to struggle with their first. As they walked by, taking their sheep to the pasture, Johnny muttered, "They make it look a lot easier than it really is."

When they were out of earshot of the boys, James said to Sam, "Think we should help them? If they'd just listen to us for a minute, we could give them some pointers. Like the more they fight with them, the more nervous and difficult the sheep get. They're both too proud to ask for help, now that they've already turned us down."

Sam laughed, "Hmmm, where do you think they got that from? Nah, let's let them figure it out. It's more art than science anyway. I think they'll get it. Let's keep an eye on them, though, just in case one of the sheep decide to pull the clippers on *them*!"

Silas and Johnny heard the men laughing and knew it was at their expense. Silas said determinedly, "Let's show them. We'll get the hang of this and be better than they are!"

They wrestled their sheep into place as best they could and began to clip them. Twenty minutes later Johnny was finished with his first sheep and led her back to the pasture proudly. When he came back to the barn his father was inspecting the wool he sheared off the sheep.

"Well, Sam," James called out to his brother. "I have some good news and some bad news. The good news is the wool is off Johnny's first sheep and it isn't even lunchtime yet! The bad news is it's already in yarn!" James held up the strips of wool sheared off the ewe to show Sam.

"Ha, ha, ha," said Johnny sarcastically.

"Seriously, Johnny. The wool needs to be in one piece so we can get a better price for it. You have to do better," Sam admonished.

When he saw the hurt look on Johnny's face, Sam walked over, put his hands on Johnny's shoulders and looked him right in the eye. "Yes, this is hard work, but you *can* do this," he stated. Sam looked at his own son, finishing his sheep. "Both of you can do this. I know you can."

With that, they all went to select their next sheep.

The morning passed quickly despite the fact there wasn't much conversation in the barn. The boys were concentrating on doing their job correctly and the men were concentrating on doing their job quickly.

Soon, Hanna brought out a basket covered with a cheery red gingham cloth. Lunch! Silas was glad he had almost finished shearing his current victim.

"I decided I'd bring some lunch down here just to keep you out of my kitchen. Ya'll stink!" Hanna declared.

She looked over the growing pile of wool on the ground. She picked up the one on top by two corners to inspect it, trying to keep the lanolin off her hands and apron.

"These look pretty good," she finally decided. "Looks like they all had healthy coats."

After the boys ran to the pump to wash their hands, she asked the men, "How are they doing?"

Sam replied, "We weren't too sure at first, but they seem to be getting in the swing of things. Their work isn't pretty, but at least they can get the wool off in one piece now."

James agreed, "Yeah, but they sure go slow! We do three or four to every one they can do. Next year maybe we should start earlier. We're not going to finish before dark tonight."

"But last year it was just the two of us, so they *are* helping," Sam pointed out. "Besides, where do you need to go?"

Sam's joke fell flat. They had temporarily forgotten they both had somewhere to go.

CHAPTER 31

Sign the Roll

President Lincoln had ordered some 30,000 troops into western Virginia because so many people in that area were undecided about their loyalties. Some of the troops had stopped in Hadley. James had been in town earlier in the week and heard the recruiters shouting, "Who will come up and sign the roll?"

He sat on the stoop outside the general store and watched as men and boys he'd known most of his life signed up to fight. He listened to the officers give their reasons for joining up with the Union Army. He wondered if they were right. He wondered if the Union would win the war. He wondered if anyone could truly *win* a war. And he wondered which of them would be coming home at the end of the war.

He watched as one of the officers gave a recruit an enlistment exam. He stood the farmer up, held him by his shoulders, swung his arms out to each side, tapped him three times on the chest, then said, "Well, if you're fit enough for farmin,' you're fit enough for soldierin.' You're in."

James stood up slowly, walked over to the table and, without a word, signed his name in the recruiting officers' roll book.

"We leave Thursday at dawn, Mr. . . . . Jackman," the officer said, turning the book so he could read it.

James nodded and turned wordlessly. He had to get home to say goodbye to his family.

CHAPTER 32

Letter From James

Union Camp
Somewhere in Virginia
May 7, 1861

> *My dearest Ruth, Johnny, Lydia, Mary and little Emily,*
> *You would hardly recognize me after these many weeks. I have not shaved since I got here. It is quite the fashion now in the Union Army for us fighting men to have beards! To be honest, it's simply so much easier not to shave. And not just us "old folks" either. Most everyone here is not yet 25 years of age.*
> *Remember Max Robertson from over near Clarksburg? He's in my company and we often talk about home and what it's like to be old around all these young whippersnappers.*
> *I hope everything is fine on the farm and you are all well. I expect you are taking excellent care of the orchard because, as you know, I want my grandkids to enjoy those trees!*
> *I know you worry about me but I don't want you to. I am in fine shape but I do miss your cooking, Ruth. We get what*

we've taken to calling "Bully Soup." It's like hot cereal, but it's cornmeal and crushed hardtack boiled in water, wine and ginger. "Hardtack" is a kind of hard bread made without yeast so it's flat and dry. The hardtack crackers they make for us could last for 300 years — that is, if the weevils and mold don't get to them first.

Some things we don't get on a regular basis and sometimes I think they are experimenting on us. Last week we were given a paste that turned out to be coffee, cream and sugar all mixed together. We were to dissolve it in water to make a cup of coffee. I'll tell you what, though, I'm stickin' to plain old coffee beans — you grind 'em, you brew 'em with some water and that's it. Plain and simple. And tastes much better.

We also get "embalmed beef" on occasion, which is just like it sounds — meat in tin cans. We are also issued salted beef. They salt it to preserve it and they say it can last two years. Problem is, we have to soak it in water all day just so we can eat it. It isn't very appealing but it keeps our minds off how bad the bugs are!

I'm sending you my pay from these last few months. I've kept some for spending with the peddlers — 'sutlers' they call them — that come to our camps. They sell things like tobacco, candy, fruit, boots and such. But their prices are scandalous! They charge <u>10 cents</u> for <u>one</u> newspaper so a few of us chip in and pass it around. But you can see, there's not much for me to spend my $13 on every month, so I'm sending you the rest. Maybe you can buy you and the girls new dresses.

You'd be surprised to see all that I have to carry with me as we move from place to place. I have a knapsack, my wool blanket, my half of a two-man tent (we button them together in the middle and the ends are left open), my groundsheet, overcoat, rifle, cartridge box, bayonet, canteen, tin cup and haversack. In my haversack (which is made of cotton fabric) I carry my eating utensils, pipe, harmonica, some food, matches, handkerchief, coin purse and my money, sewing kit, my Bible, pictures of you, my *letter writing kit, tobacco pouch, and an ingenious spiked candle holder. I just stick it in the ground when I need a light to read by or like now when I'm writing to you. And just in case you think I have it easy for having all these helpful utensils — remember, I have to carry it all. It weighs about 50 pounds when it's all loaded up! And our uniforms weigh another seven pounds or so — and they're wool. Sometimes I sweat so much that I'm afraid I'll turn into a big smelly puddle one of these days.*

I haven't seen much fighting yet, and it's often quite boring for us. We do get training most every day. When our instructor was showing us about the muskets, he told us it was just like hunting squirrels, only these squirrels had guns. We also play cards and read. We pass around any books or newspapers we can find. It's so boring that sometimes we'll read an old newspaper and pretend it's new.

There are many interesting men here in my company, from all over the north. It goes to show how big this country of ours is. The men come from all different backgrounds, which is a benefit to us all. If anything breaks, there is always someone who can fix it. We even have men here who immigrated from Canada, England, Germany and Ireland. They say they came to our country for their freedom and because this is the land of opportunity. They want to help preserve that so they've joined our fight.

My candle is burning low now and I must get some sleep. Please do not worry about me. I am well and in good spirits and trust in my usual good luck. I shall use all the caution and courage I am capable of and leave the rest to take care of itself. I will see you all soon. We don't hear much news of the war, but it would seem it won't last much longer.

Your loving husband and father,
James

CHAPTER 33

Estrangement

Hanna could not let go of the argument she had with Ruth back in May when their husbands decided to go fight. Even though it had been several months, the horrible words they shouted at each other would pop into her head at the most unexpected moments. Tonight, she was washing the dishes and suddenly heard Ruth call Sam a lunkhead. Her own response to Ruth echoed in her memory.

"Never come back . . . ." Hanna said quietly to no one in particular.

"What did you say, Ma?" asked Elizabeth.

Hanna looked at her children.

Silas was trying to master the wooden game he got from Santa Claus last Christmas. It was a wooden cup on a handle with a wooden ball attached to it by a string. The object was to get the ball into the cup.

Hanna decided it must be harder than it looked, based on the frustration on her son's face. "He'd be better at it if he could play more instead of having to work so much," she thought sadly.

Elizabeth and Abigail were having a tea party with their dolls.

"Nothing. I was just talking to myself," Hanna replied, turning back to her dishes.

She thought about her husband and wondered if he was safe. Then she wondered about James. Was he safe, too? This led her to think about Ruth and the children. In a small town like Hadley, she would have heard if there were any problems. But she still wondered.

"This is stupid," she thought, suddenly angry with herself. "Not only are we family, but we are business partners!"

This was to be the year their "dual farm proposition" was to pay off. In these years since Grandpa died, Sam and James have worked so hard to make both the sheep and the orchard prosper.

Hanna wondered how the orchard was doing and if Johnny and Ruth were able to handle the work. At least the sheep shearing was done and the profit divided between the two families. The same will have to be done with the apple harvest, assuming all is going well with the orchard.

Hanna sighed. She knew she should stop this quarrel with Ruth, but it has been so many months. Each day that went by made it more difficult to end it.

"What if I go to Ruth and she slams the door in my face? I'm just not strong enough," she concluded to herself. "I hope the boys are."

CHAPTER 34

Letter from Sam

Confederate Camp
Somewhere in South Carolina

My dearest Hanna, Silas, Elizabeth and Abigail,
> *I miss you all so much! I hope you are well and you children are helping your mother take care of everything while I'm away.*
> *I have a few minutes so I thought I would take some time to write a few words home. Maybe that will make camp seem more like home.*
> *You wouldn't believe how many bugs are around camp — flies, mosquitos, fleas. The hardtack we get almost always has bugs in it. It's not unusual that when I dip my hardtack in my coffee, the surface is immediately covered with weevils. The first time it happened, I poured my coffee out, but after that I realized I'd never get any coffee again. And you know how much I love my coffee! I tried not dunking my hardtack in my coffee, but I about*

broke off my teeth trying to eat it. "Hardtack" is surely a fitting name for it. Now I just skim the bugs off the top and drink it down.

Yesterday for entertainment we had lice races. A louse is a bug that attaches to you or an animal and sucks your blood. When I first saw them, I tried everything to get rid of them, but then I realized they were everywhere and gave up. We gathered up a few of them and put them on the flat side of a canteen and wagered which one would get to the other side first. We had quite a good time with that. I won eighteen cents, too!

Another thing we do for fun here is play baseball. We don't have balls or bats, but we can always find a good stick. We wrap a walnut with yarn or a strip of cloth to make the ball. We can play for hours when it's not too hot.

Now as I reread this letter, it will seem as if I don't do much of anything, which is far from the truth. This is what our typical day looks like:

Reveille at 5 a.m.
Breakfast Call at 7 a.m.
Guard Mounting at 9 a.m.
Dinner Call at noon
Company Drills from 1 - 3 p.m.
Dress Parade at 6 p.m.
Supper at 7 p.m.
Tattoo at 9 p.m. (Calls us to our tents for the night)
Taps at 10 p.m.

And when we're not doing any of that, there are camp chores to do. (I can hear you children laughing at me, havin' somebody tell me to do chores just like I tell you to do yours.) We have to build roads, dig trenches for latrines, take care of the horses and mules, and fix equipment. And if we draw wood cutting or water detail, sometimes we're away from camp for days. The wood in most of our camps has already been scavenged for firewood or what-have-you so we have to take a wagon and go pretty far away to find some. And even when we're able to camp near a river, the water is *rarely clean enough for drinking. We always have to go find clean drinking water.*

So, don't think I just sit around all day. I am busy even though we haven't seen much fighting. I expect this war to end soon; maybe I'll never see any fighting. I don't want you to worry about me. I promise to take good care of myself if you promise the same.

Until we see each other again —
Your loving father and husband,

Samuel

CHAPTER 35

Sick Sheep

Silas lay in his comfortable bed, listening to the crowing of the rooster. He was tired. He missed his father. He didn't want to get up before the sun each day and work until he dropped into bed, too exhausted to eat his supper.

As he lay there, he could almost imagine how it used to be. He closed his eyes and could hear his father's low, deep voice talking to his mother as she made breakfast. He could smell the rich aroma of the coffee perking on the stove.

Since his father had been gone, his mother didn't make coffee any more. She would boil a little water for the single cup of tea she'd have with her breakfast. She said it was because she never liked coffee, but Silas knew it was to save money, even if it was just a few pennies.

Sometimes his mother and father would have breakfast by themselves, without waking the children. Silas especially liked those mornings. He could pick up the current book he was reading and lose himself in it before the day even began.

By contrast, his *least* favorite time was when he was reading at night and his ma or pa hollered up at him, "Silas, blow that candle out! Do you think they grow on trees? We're not made of money, y'know!"

If he was very lucky, there wouldn't be an enormous amount of work to do on the farm that day and his parents would linger over their breakfast together. On those days, he always hoped that Abigail and Elizabeth would stay in their beds and be quiet, too. It was such a comfortable, safe time.

His reverie was broken, though, by his mother calling up to him. "Silas, time for breakfast! Wake the girls!"

As they were eating, his mother asked, "Silas, what do you need to do today?"

Let's see, Silas thought. I need to go fishin' for awhile, then take a swim in the pond, then maybe read some more . . . .

Silas thought for a moment, then groaned. "I've got to bale that hay and get it up in the barn."

"We'll help!" yelled Elizabeth.

"Yeah!" piped up little Abigail.

Silas looked at them wistfully and said, "I wish you could. But it's too hard."

Their faces both fell. "Pa would let us. I wish he was here," Abbey said sadly.

"I'll tell you what. You come out there after I've been working for awhile and bring me a big pail of icy cold water. Then we'll see if there's anything you can help with. Okay?" Silas reached over and gave one of Abbey's braids a gentle yank.

Both girls smiled at their big brother.

Silas's mother turned away so they wouldn't see the fat tear rolling down her face. Hanna had conflicting emotions. She was so proud of the way Silas was handling himself and the farm while his father was away, but she felt guilty and angry, too.

You're right, Abbey. I wish Pa was here too, she said

— 147 —

silently.

Out in the yard Silas looked at the huge pile of hay. "It didn't seem that big yesterday. I think it grew over night," he said to Tosh, who had run up to him. "I don't quite know where to start."

Silas tried to remember what his father did when it was time to bale the hay, but Tosh began barking at him.

"Be quiet, would you? I'm tryin' to think," Silas told her, but Tosh kept barking expectantly.

Silas looked at her. This was not a playful bark. She wanted something. "What is it?" he asked her.

Knowing she got Silas' attention, she ran off and stopped twenty feet away, looking to see if he was following. Silas knew enough to follow and to be concerned. Tosh was smart and took care of the sheep very well. Something was wrong with one of them.

Silas followed Tosh to the feeding shed in the middle of the pasture. The small log building was used in the winter when they had to put out food for the sheep. It also gave them shelter from bad weather.

"Why would Tosh bring me here?" wondered Silas. "There's plenty of grazing and not a storm in sight."

Then Silas heard it. Quiet bleating was coming from the shed. One of the sheep must be sick, he thought, alarmed. As he turned the corner, he stopped dead in his tracks.

"Oh, no! There must be thirty sheep in here!" Silas' heart quit beating for a moment and he began to sweat. Then he collected himself, saying, "Okay, let's figure this out. What's wrong?"

Bending over the nearest ewe, he stuck a finger in her mouth like his father showed him. "Please be warm, please be warm, please be warm," prayed Silas.

It was ice cold. He tried another, it was cold too. All these sheep were sick!

"Uh oh," said Silas to Tosh.

What was wrong with them? Were the rest sick too? Where were the others? Are they dying? What should he do? Silas's mind flooded with questions. He couldn't think. He was beginning to panic.

What would his father say? That jolted him back to reality.

His father would say what he always said, "Keep a cool head. Use all of your senses. Look around. Really *see* the problem. Listen. Touch them. They'll tell you what's wrong if you let them."

Silas stopped and looked around. He saw the sheep lying on their sides in the cool of the shed. He heard their desperate bleating. He already knew their mouths were cold. He took a deep breath to calm himself the rest of the way. That's when he realized the shed smelled worse than normal. Sheep aren't normally rose scented, but this was much worse than normal.

"Ma! Ma! I have to get Doc Perkins!" Silas yelled as he ran by the kitchen door.

When Silas rode back in the doctor's wagon, he saw his mother and sisters out in the shed with the sheep. Doc Perkins climbed down from the wagon, nodded to Hanna as he hurried by, then knelt by one of the ewes in the shed. He stuck a finger in her mouth. "Yup, just like you said, young'un. Where's your Pa?"

"Gone to war. They're my responsibility. What's wrong with them?" Silas was trying to hurry the old doctor along with his diagnosis.

"Hold your horses, boy, let me look at them."

The old veterinarian poked and prodded the ewe, then put his big weathered hands around her stomach. The pathetic sheep jumped and groaned.

"Got yourself some parasites, boy."

"What's that?" asked Silas, worried.

Doc Perkins explained, "They're little worms that get

inside the sheep and attach to their stomach lining and their intestines. They feed on the sheep's blood and other fluids. They'll kill the whole flock if you don't stop them."

Silas's mind raced. He had a million more questions. He asked, "What do I . . . how do I . . . what if . . . "

"You have a lot of questions, don't you?" the doctor laughed. "How 'bout if I just tell you I have some medicine you need to give them, and you need to keep them away from that pond until it clears. I have something for you to put in the water to kill whatever's in there. That's probably where they got the worms."

Silas's face turned ashen and he had to lean against the wall of the shed to keep from falling over. He remembered that day in March when his father told him to clear the pond of weeds and muck so the water didn't foul.

He didn't do it the day they talked about it because of the excitement with the newborn lambs. He promised his father he'd do it the next day. But he didn't. He didn't forget — he remembered he needed to do it. He had every intention of doing it. But he didn't. There was always something more interesting to do.

Silas wanted to sink right into the ground and never come up. He had let everyone down because of his selfishness and laziness. And now looked what happened!

"Don't take it so hard, boy! I told you I had some medicine to give them. They'll be fine in a couple weeks. You caught it in time. You should be proud you're taking such good care of things while your Pa's away," the old doctor clapped his hand firmly on Silas's shoulder, then began rummaging through his black bag. "Ah, there it is."

Silas felt even worse. Being praised for catching the problem that he caused in the first place. And having to pay money they didn't even have for medicine they shouldn't even need. It was almost more than he could bear.

Silas noticed his mother talking quietly to Doc

Perkins as they walked to his wagon.

As Silas walked up, he saw the bottle in his mother's hand then heard her say, "Yes, money's been tight, but I do appreciate your offer. I'll measure you tomorrow when you come out. And thank you."

Doc Perkins climbed into the wagon and took hold of the reins. "I told your mother how much to give them based on their weight. I'll stop by tomorrow and check on them, and bring you some more. Find the rest of them to make sure no others are infected." To Hanna he said, "You've got the makings of a fine sheep rancher, there, ma'am. See you tomorrow." He slapped his horse lightly with the reins, commanded, "Git! C'mon, Chippy, let's go!" and off they trotted.

Hanna looked at her son and said lightly, "Well, this doesn't seem so bad, does it? To pay for the medicine, I'm going to knit him a wool sweater for the winter."

Silas couldn't look her in the eye so he turned and began to walk toward the pond. "I'll go put a fence around the pond, then round up the rest of the sheep."

Hanna watched him curiously until he was out of sight.

CHAPTER 36

Letter From Sam

Confederate Camp
Somewhere in South Carolina
June 17, 1861

My Dearest Hanna, Silas, Elizabeth, and Abbey,
  *Oh, I miss you all so much. There are other things I miss
as well. I miss my bed. I am sleeping in a tent with 23 other
men. It's so crowded that when one of us turns over in our sleep,
all of us have to.*
  *I'm supposed to get $11 in Confederate money each
month in pay, but none of us has seen any wages for awhile.
The last time I sent you any money was the last time we got
paid. I hope what I sent before will see you through until I
receive some more. For my wages I am required to live in
crowded camps with more men than I ever imagined, march
in step for hours at a time, follow every order that the
commanders can think of (sometimes I think they just make
up odd rules to see if we'll obey them), eat army food without*

complaint (although I guess I am complaining now!), try not to get sick, and do my best to avoid the incredible boredom of camp life.

I am one of the oldest men here, most are in their 20s, but some are just boys. No one really knows their true age. Many of them are so anxious to join the fray that they go to great lengths to get in the military. I was talking to one boy last week who didn't look much older than you, Silas. He told me his Ma and Pa and the Good Book always taught him not to tell lies so he wrote "18" on a scrap of paper and put it in his shoe. When he talked to the recruiting officer about joining up he felt he could honestly say, "I'm _over_ 18." I told him that was steppin' pretty close to the valley of fibbin' and I hoped he didn't fall over the edge one day.

Let me tell you about my tent, now that we're somewhat settled here in camp. It's a large canvas cone about 12 feet tall and 18 feet around the base. There is a tall pole sticking up the center with an opening in the top. When it rains, though, we have to close the flap and I'll tell you what! Remember when that skunk tangled with the dogs last summer? When we have to close up our tent it smells worse in here than the perfume from that lonesome polecat. Let's just say that some of the men here have a problem with their personal grooming — they stink up the place! (They probably are telling their families the same thing about me.) Our tent sleeps a dozen men comfortably so of course the army puts about 20 men in here! We sleep with our feet toward the middle to make more space, but it's very crowded. I understand that they copied the design from the Indians out west.

You should see me when we move camp. I never thought I'd have to carry everything I own on my back. It took me awhile to get this right, but I roll up my blanket and ground sheet and wrap it around my extra clothes. Then I sling it across my shoulder and tie it around my waist. I also wear my rifle, my leather cartridge box, my bayonet in the scabbard, my canteen and my *cotton haversack. I look like a mule all packed up for a trip! In my haversack I carry my razor, towel, soap, comb, jackknife, writing kit, my mess kit with a tin plate, tin cup, fork, knife and spoon (I'll give you one guess why they call it a "mess" kit!), that little Bible you gave me before I left, pictures of you, my change purse and what little money I have, a handkerchief, my sewing kit (yes, I have to do my own women's work), my tobacco pouch, matches and my pipe. It's actually quite remarkable that we can carry around so much of the items that make our lives a little easier, but this can weigh 50 pounds. And you know how old and feeble I am.*

Now let me tell you about the food I have to endure. We make what we call our "Confederate Cush." It's a stew of bacon, cornbread and water that we boil until the water is all gone. It fills the stomach but please don't make this for me when I get home! Sometimes I just let my mind wander back to your kitchen, Hanna, and on a good day (when I'm not downwind of the camp), I can almost taste your roast chicken and sweet potato pie and that special bread you make with the onions. Then I top it off with a big slab of your chocolate cake and I can almost endure the dinner I expect Cookie will make for us. You think I'm joking, but yesterday when I broke my cornbread (which we get at every meal), it was so moldy it looked like it had cobwebs in it. We get so desperate for things we don't have that we've taken to experimenting with what we have plenty of. Coffee, for instance. You know how I like my coffee morning, noon and night. Well, we can't get hardly any coffee. But we have bushels of peanuts and potatoes so we tried to make coffee from those. Didn't work too well, though, so tomorrow we're tryin' some corn and maybe some chicory we found. We're keepin' our fingers crossed. And when I get home, I'll be drinkin' coffee right out of the pot.

We did get some real coffee last week, but it's already gone. It's the darnedest story. Some of us were in the woods near camp collecting some firewood when we came to a small stream. Across the stream we could see a Union camp. It was obvious they were relaxing before dinner because we could hear some fiddle player and some singin' and we could smell the coffee! 'Bout that same time they saw us and we all stared at each other. Finally, a man in our company hollered across to them, "You got any coffee to spare?" Next thing we knew here comes a little paper sailboat like I taught the boys to make last year with a little tin of coffee sittin' on it like a passenger ridin' the ferry. While we were fetchin' it out of the water, we hear them yell "Got any tobacco?" So we all dug into our pockets and sent the sailboat back with a cargo of tobacco.

When we were walkin' back to camp afterward, a man who recently joined our company told us that, where he was before, they were close by a Union camp like this and one night they practically had a sing-along. The Union troops began singin' songs from the South and the Confederates would respond with songs from the North.

I know it seems strange since technically I guess we're enemies, but there is a certain brotherhood out here with us all and, of course, I do think of James quite often and wonder how he's gettin' on wherever he is. I think most of us are really just fighting to protect our traditions and to be left alone to live our lives. I don't think any of us truly believe killin' somebody is the way to solve these problems. If it was up to us instead of the officers, we probably could have this whole thing settled in half an hour over one of your chicken dinners.

But enough of this complaining. I haven't seen much battle and for that I'm glad. The closest I've come to fighting is making what we call "Quaker guns." You remember the Zanes, used to live past the creek? They were Quakers — didn't believe in fighting. Well, we make these fake cannons out of big logs and paint them to look real so when the Yanks *look out at a field covered in these, they might think twice about tanglin' with us Rebs.*

I am running out of candle for tonight, so I must close this letter. I miss you all and would love to see you and hold you. But until I get back, I'll just have to hold on to my memories and look forward to the day we can be together again. I hope the farm isn't too much for you to handle. I often wonder if I've done the right thing and can only ask God to help me and forgive me as He sees fit.

Your loving husband and father,
Sam

Chapter 37

Moths

Late summer was hot and humid. It was the kind of weather that makes a person want to sit down with a cold glass of lemonade and never get up again. At least that's the fantasy Johnny was having.

He was worried about drought. There had not been a drop of rain for three weeks. The orchard was looking bad. The trees could survive without water for awhile, but when they get stressed, they are more prone to insect infestations and disease. But even if the trees survive the lack of rainfall, their apples were likely to be dwarfed, bringing a much lower price than they'd need to break even this year. All Johnny could do was watch the sky and pray for rain.

He began to walk out to the orchard to take a closer look. He stooped and pulled a long piece of yellow orchard grass and put the end in his mouth, like he'd seen his father do a thousand times. As he walked, he looked around at all the orchard grass he still had to cut. He tried to do a bit each day, but didn't always get around to this particularly unpleasant chore. He constantly heard his Uncle Sam's voice in his head saying, "Don't put off till tomorrow what you can do today."

Johnny chuckled out loud at the memory of the last time he heard Sam speak those words to Silas. Johnny had been standing behind Uncle Sam so that as Sam spoke to Silas, Sam couldn't see the silly faces Johnny was making. Johnny was mimicking Sam as Sam lectured Silas about something or other, rolling his eyes and generally being goofy, trying to make Silas laugh. Silas was in complete control, though, and did not laugh. He must have given some indication of what was happening behind his father's back because suddenly Sam whirled around, just in time to see one of Johnny's ridiculous faces.

The only problem was Johnny's eyes were closed so he didn't know he'd been caught! He continued making fun of his uncle up until the time Sam grabbed him by his upper arm and pulled him into the barn where he deposited a shovel into Johnny's hand.

"Here, let's see if you think mucking out the sheep shed is as funny as bein' disrespectful to your elders!" Sam said harshly as he stomped away.

Later, Silas told Johnny that his pa was not nearly as angry as he led the boys to believe. Silas had overheard his father tell his mother about the incident. Sam had told her that he could barely keep from laughing because it was exactly what he and James had done to their father thirty years earlier.

"The apple doesn't fall far from the tree!" he had said at the time.

Johnny was still chuckling as he reached the first row of apple trees. But then he stopped. This was definitely not something to laugh about.

The apples didn't look right — they had something on them.

Johnny ran back to the barn to get a ladder so he could inspect them more closely. As he climbed up higher into the tree, he got a bad feeling in the pit of his stomach. He reached for the apple closest to him and saw what he had been dreading. He saw larvae from the codling moth on the apples! The larvae feed on the pulp from the apples. When they've had just enough to ruin the apples, they turn into tiny moths and fly away.

For years his father had been trying to get the orchard to produce apples. Now that it has, it could be destroyed by a little moth.

Johnny didn't know what to do; this situation had never come up before. He stood for the longest time on the ladder staring at the apple in his hand.

He tried to brush the larvae off the apple but it was sticky and on tight. He tried to flick it off with his finger, but, again, it was stuck fast. As he flicked, though, he lost his balance on the ladder and grabbed tight to the apple on the branch for support.

Squish. The larvae squirted off the apple and on to his shirt.

"Oh, bleah!" Johnny grimaced in distaste. "Yuck!"

Suddenly, Johnny knew what he had to do but he was not happy about it. He climbed down the ladder and ran toward the house.

"Ma! Ma! I need a couple of rags to take out to the orchard!" he shouted.

"What is all this ruckus?" Ruth met Johnny on the porch, wiping her hands on her apron. "What do you need rags for?" his mother asked.

"Uh . . . well . . . you don't really want to know, Ma," replied Johnny.

" 'Uh . . . well' . . . yes I do. You've piqued my curiosity, m'boy. Now I'll get your rags just as soon as you tell me what you're up to." Ruth was a tough customer and

Johnny knew it.

Johnny heaved a sigh. "I have to squish the moths on the trees. I need the rags to wipe the goo off the apples."

"Eeeeewwwww!" Ruth wrinkled her nose and looked oddly at her son for a moment. "I can't think of a better solution to this disgusting problem. Here," she said, handing Johnny a towel hanging by the door. "I'll bring you a couple more in a little while. Do you need any help?"

Johnny thought for a minute. This was the woman who prepared their food every day . . . "Nah, I'll do it myself. You keep your hands clean." As he was jumping off the porch, he called out, "I may not be too hungry for supper, though."

Back in the orchard, Johnny climbed the ladder again. As he looked closer, he was able to see that not every apple had a parasite on it. Regardless, it was still a lot of goo to remove from a lot of apples. He got busy.

After a few hours of *squish — wipe — squish — wipe*, he finished the first row of trees. Then he moved the ladder to the second row. As he climbed, he was surprised and more than a little pleased to find not a single larvae on these apples. He flew down the ladder and moved it to the next tree, practically running to the top.

Inspecting the apples, he yelled, "Yippee!"

His mother came running to the orchard. "What is it?" she asked, out of breath.

"They haven't infested the other trees. I'm finished! Now I can come out here every day and inspect the trees. I can keep ahead of these stupid moths." Johnny was dancing around his mother, ecstatic that he solved the problem and could be done with this revolting chore. He grabbed his mother's hands and began to twirl her around. They were laughing and being silly, now that the potential crisis had passed.

Suddenly his mother withdrew her hands from his and stopped twirling.

"Eww . . . have you washed your hands?" she wrinkled her nose again.

Johnny ran off toward the pump, laughing. "Don't worry, Ma! I'll get 'em real clean."

"You better! And leave that shirt outside — no bug guts in my house," she warned shrilly.

CHAPTER 38

Wolves

Silas was exhausted. He had not slept properly in three nights. He realized with dismay there was always something to occupy his mind. Now that the sheep were healthy again, he had something different to worry about. The tainted water didn't kill any sheep, but now some predator was terrorizing the animals. They had lost one ewe and three lambs already.

The first night, Tuesday, Tosh was barking and barking hysterically, so Silas hurried outside with his father's gun. With clouds covering the moon, he couldn't see a thing.

In the morning, there were two lambs missing.

Wednesday night the moon was bright so when Tosh barked a warning, Silas felt confident he'd fix whatever was lurking out there. But he was wrong. He could feel the presence of something, but did not see it.

In the morning, an ewe and a lamb were missing.

"What are we going to do?" Silas lamented to his

mother. "At this rate, we won't have any sheep by the end of summer. And what if this wolf, or whatever is doing this, tells all his buddies what easy pickin's we have here? What will we do then?"

Silas was very worried. He wasn't nearly good enough with the gun to take on a pack of wolves. He really wasn't even good enough to take on a pack of turtles, but he pushed that thought from his mind.

His mother walked over to the kitchen chair where Silas sat and stroked his dark hair. "You'll figure it out. In fact, you can mull it over while you go into town. I need a few things from Mr. Hawkins."

His mother's confidence in him gave him the boost he needed to quit whining and start solving this problem.

"Okay, Ma. I'll let my brain do the thinkin' while my feet do the stinkin'!" said Silas with a laugh.

Hanna laughed. "Get out of here and take your bad poetry with you." She gave him a push toward the door and put her grocery list in his hand.

"Tell Mr. Hawkins you need to put it on the account — and don't be too long," she hollered after him.

When Silas got to Hawkins General Store, he tried to climb all four stairs with one step. Two weeks ago he was only able to take three stairs at a time, so he was trying to beat his own record.

"Way to go, Silas."

Silas turned toward the sound of the familiar voice. He saw Johnny leaning against the wall at the bottom of the stairs.

"Thanks," mumbled Silas, unsure if he was being teased or not.

"I got all four in one step today, too," said Johnny.

They stood for a moment in an uncomfortable silence. The door to Hawkins' store swung out and almost hit Silas. He moved down the steps out of Mrs. Montgomery's way.

"You here for your ma, too?" asked Silas.

"Yep," answered Johnny.

More uncomfortable silence. Then they both spoke at once.

"Well, I gotta . . ."

"Howsit goin' out . . ."

They tried again.

"Oh, go ahead . . ."

"What were you sayin' . . ."

The cousins both laughed in embarrassment at their predicament. They had spoken millions of words to each other in their lifetimes, but felt like they had just met.

"You first," said Johnny.

"I was just going to ask how you were doing with the orchard," replied Silas.

Johnny explained with all the gory details — and using all the appropriate facial expressions — of his problem with the codling moths.

"Eeeeewwwww," groaned Silas when Johnny finished with his story.

Johnny laughed. "That's just what my mother said. How are the sheep?"

Silas began telling Johnny the problems he was having. When he finished, he said angrily, "I am sick of having so many problems to fix every day. If it's not sick sheep, it's having to bale hay, or it's a broken fence, or it's these stupid wolves! I'm sick of it!"

"I know," Johnny said. "I can't believe the work I have to do every day and I still don't get it all done. Here it is the end of August and I still don't have the orchard grass cut. It's not fair!"

They both sat on Hawkins' bottom step and took turns complaining about their lives.

Finally, Silas said, "I hate my pa for leaving."

He was instantly sorry when he saw Johnny's eyes widen in surprise. "I . . . I . . . I didn't mean that. And don't tell anyone I said that."

Johnny looked him straight in the eye and said, "You said it and you meant it." Silas looked at the ground in shame. "But I feel the exact same way."

The two boys sat there, now in a comfortable silence, each thinking about what the other had said.

"It must be wrong to be so angry at my pa, but I've tried and I can't help it. He didn't *have* to go and leave us here by ourselves for so long. He *wanted* to!" said Silas in a rush.

"I know. It's hard to be proud of what he's doing when it makes it so bad for us here. Well, for me, anyway. No one else has to work this hard. The girls don't do anything all day, except a few chores for Ma in the house. Not like what I have to do," Johnny spat out the last four words.

Both boys were ashamed of their feelings about their fathers and their situations. For too long, they had been feeling sorry for themselves, which led them to anger, which led them to guilt, which led them to confusion and back to feeling sorry for themselves. It was an ugly circle that bound them tightly.

Their feelings were overwhelming and too large to fix so Silas changed the subject.

Silas looked sheepishly at his cousin. "I have to get these things for Ma then get back home. And I still haven't figured out what to do about keeping the sheep safe!" he lamented.

"Have you tried staying out there at night so you can see what's doing it?" Johnny asked helpfully.

Silas looked at Johnny. "That's a great idea. That's just what I'll do. Thanks!" he said, relieved to have a potential solution. He wished, though, that Johnny could stay with him in the pasture. But he knew neither of their mothers would want them to do that, what with their special family situation.

"Bye."

"Bye."

Silas ran up the steps. As Johnny was walking away he heard, "Mr. Hawkins! Are you here? My ma needs some things and she's waiting for me."

CHAPTER 39

Showdown

Thursday night, Silas took Johnny's advice and camped out with the sheep. His mother was not happy with the idea, but she sent him out with plenty of blankets in case it got chilly and some bread with jam to snack on. She had even brewed him some coffee and gave it to him with his dinner.

"This always helps your Pa stay awake," she told him.

Silas didn't have the heart to tell her he'd really rather have an icy cold glass of milk instead of the bitter black brew.

"Oh well, it won't kill me," he thought to himself, taking a drink. He made a face he hoped his mother didn't see. "On the other hand, it just might!"

After he got settled into his temporary bedroom with his roommates — that is, some meadow grass and a bunch of noisy sheep — he planned his attack on whatever came looking for trouble tonight.

He looked around in the dark. It was dark, not much moon. Johnny sat very still listening to the night sounds.

What was that? He heard a noise nearby. He tried to

find where the noise came from but could see nothing.

What was that? Another noise from behind him made him jump. He turned around but again saw nothing.

An uneasy feeling came over him. How many animals were watching him right now? Suddenly, he wanted nothing more than to be in his warm, bright house with his Ma. He even thought it wouldn't be so bad to be little again so he could sit on her lap. It was all he could do to keep from running all the way back to the house.

He shook his head violently to clear these thoughts from his head.

"Maybe I'll have a little snack," he thought, so he ate a piece of the homemade bread with jam spread all the way to the edges, just the way he liked it. Unfortunately, a full stomach and a couple nights of empty sleep conspired against Silas. He began to nod off. After several minutes of his head bobbing down to his chest and then jerking awake, he gave up. He pulled the soft blankets around and under him, making himself a cozy little nest.

Suddenly, Tosh began barking right in his ear. Silas leapt up out of his makeshift bed, tripping over his own feet. He fell, got up, then tripped over a blanket. All the while, Tosh was barking and growling fiercely off in the distance.

Finally, Silas was standing. The moon had come out and he looked around. There it was — a wolf on the prowl. The majestic animal was standing at the edge of the meadow. As the moon danced in and out of the clouds, Silas saw the wolf raise his head. A mournful, spooky howl filled the still night air.

The hair on the back of Silas' neck stood at attention.

The lambs ran frantically around their mothers, hoping for protection they couldn't provide.

Silas said a quick prayer as he picked up his father's gun. "Dear Lord, I know I've been feelin' sorry for myself lately, but if I don't get rid of this critter . . ." He couldn't finish because he was concentrating, trying to remember everything Pa had told him about shooting a gun.

He remembered the episode with the bear that charged them and Silas immediately calmed down. "Pa was right!" he thought. "I'm not so scared this time. I'll just do what I need to do."

He had learned the lesson about keeping his gun loaded in situations like these and was glad he hadn't had an ugly mishap when he tripped over the blanket.

He put his eye to the sight, bracing the butt of the rifle against his shoulder. He knew if he needed more than one shot, the predator would be gone and he'd have to be out here again tomorrow night. He held his breath and aimed. Just as he pulled the trigger, the moon again danced behind a cloud.

BLAM!

The rifle pounded him in the shoulder and knocked him down. It felt like a log was thrown at him. Silas struggled to get up, holding his shoulder in pain. He tried to see in the dark, but couldn't. Tosh was barking frantically but Silas couldn't see her.

He followed the sound of her bark and almost tripped over her in the dark. The cloud moved away from the moon and his eyes began to adjust. He stood in the meadow, straining his eyes to see.

Over there! Tosh! He went to her. She was standing over the dead body of a silvery gray wolf. Silas stood over it for a long while, too. He knew it had to be done and that he had done the right thing, but he couldn't feel jubilant about killing this beautiful animal. He didn't even feel like celebrating the fact that he only needed one shot, even in the dark.

As he turned toward the house and his comfortable bed, he said, "I'm sorry, guy. It was you or my sheep. And you've had enough of my sheep."

CHAPTER 40

Reconciliation

After a peaceful night's sleep, his first in several nights, Silas stretched and assessed his situation.

"I've lost two ewes and four lambs, but if that was the renegade wolf and he's dead, then maybe we can get back to normal around here," Silas thought to himself.

He relived the events of the previous week, ending with his shooting of the majestic wolf. He was so weary last night he hadn't bothered to dispose of the carcass. He'd have to do that today.

"I wonder if Johnny . . ." Silas thought his cousin might be interested in knowing his suggestion worked. Maybe he'd even want to see the dead wolf. Maybe they could quit being mad at each other. Silas tried hard to remember why they, and their mothers, were not speaking. But it all seemed like a lifetime ago.

Suddenly Silas leapt out of bed and threw on his clothes. He couldn't do anything about the women fighting, but he could sure do something to make himself feel better.

Through the house he ran, grabbing a thick slice of bread off the plate in his startled mothers' hands, calling, "No time for breakfast, Ma! Stuff to do! Oh, I got the wolf!"

He ended up in the orchard, slowing to catch his breath. Off in the distance he saw Worthy McKay working with the beehives.

A flash of memory clouded his eyes. The pages of his life moved backward as if ruffled by a breeze, until they stopped at the horrible memory of what had happened at Worthy McKay's honey house. Even though Rooster and Toad actually caused the damage, Silas knew deep down that he and Johnny had the power to stop them but didn't. He still felt ashamed.

"Hey!" Johnny called to Silas, jolting him from his memories.

"Hey, yourself," Silas responded, walking up to where Johnny was working.

They both stared at their feet, not quite knowing what to say.

Finally Silas looked up and said, "Can we go back like we were before?"

Smiling, Johnny said, "I was hoping that's why you came."

Relieved, Silas sighed. "I also wanted to tell you I took your advice and got that wolf last night. You want to see it?"

"Do I! Let's go!"

As they ran back the way Silas had just come, he glimpsed Worthy McKay again and slowed down. Johnny turned to where Silas was looking and turned away again fast.

He confided in Silas, "Every time he comes here I can't even look at him I'm so ashamed."

"Yeah, I was just thinking about that day," Silas agreed.

They walked in silence through the beautiful orchard so alive with the late summer colors, sounds and smells.

Suddenly Silas stopped. "I know. Remember how awful Worthy's porch was?" Johnny nodded. "Let's fix it. He'll be here for awhile and he won't know we did it."

Johnny turned and began to run toward his barn. "I'll get some boards and my tools and meet you there. Bring some nails — I don't have any extras," he called over his shoulder.

Silas was already on his way.

When Silas got to the honey house, Johnny was already there. He had loaded up their wagon with some of the lumber he was to use on the apple cellar. When he saw Silas' questioning eyes, Johnny said, "It's alright. I'll get more later. Better yet, maybe I'll just make the apple cellar smaller!"

They both laughed and got right to work because they didn't want to be there when Worthy McKay came back.

Two hours later, hot and thirsty, the boys stepped back and admired their work. It was a brand new solid porch with no holes — not even any rough spots. They felt proud of themselves.

"Now maybe I can look him in the eye when he comes to care for the hives," said Johnny.

Silas smiled and nodded, then they began to load up the wagon.

As the boys rode back toward the orchard, Worthy McKay stepped around the side of his honey house and wiped away a tear.

CHAPTER **41**

Letter From Martha

Atlanta, Georgia
August 5, 1861

Dear Ruth and children,
*I received your most unhappy news that James and Sam
have both gone off to fight in this war between the states. It is an
ugly business down here in the South also.*
*My William, however, has paid $300 for a substitute to
fight for him. It's common here to do that. I have heard that at
least 50,000 Southern gentlemen have done so. But don't think
it's because they're not willing to die for their beliefs or that they're
yellow. It's just that it's absolutely necessary to keep them here to
run things.*
*By happy coincidence, I've recently heard from our
brothers, Charles and Thomas. Charles says he is busier than ever
in Baltimore. He writes that because the Yanks need so many
uniforms, he has doubled the number of sewing machines in his
factory. I expect he will get rich because of this war.*

Thomas, too, is doing well financially these days. At his blacksmith shop, he does not repair much farm equipment anymore. Now he has had to hire a man to help him build and repair military equipment, of all things. He too, I think, will become wealthy from this war.

Oh, Ruth, I am so sorry to sound so callous about all this. As I read what I've written so far, I see that it must not cheer you up, as was my intention. I know you must miss James and are probably terribly worried about James and Sam. I am, too.

But don't you worry. I've read in the papers that this will all be over shortly and everyone will be home where they belong. We can get our lives back to normal then!

I will end this note now, hoping it has somewhat lifted your spirits. We will have another visit like we did last Christmas when this is all behind us.

I hope the children are healthy and you are handling the farm without too much trouble.

With Love,
Martha

CHAPTER 42

Letter From James

Union Camp
Somewhere in Virginia
July 21, 1861

My dearest family,
*   I am writing this letter because I was thinking of you and desperately want to be home in our little farmhouse with you.*
*   Yesterday was the worst day of my life, without a doubt. I saw my first true battle and the horror of it will be with me forever. Normally, I wouldn't worry you with war news like this, but everyone must know how truly awful it is. Maybe this war will be the last, when everyone realizes what a toll it takes.*
*   We met the Confederates on a battlefield near Bull Run Creek over by Manassas Junction. It's hilly country here with lots of places to hide and many places where you can't see very far. We all carry Henry repeating rifles. We joke that we can load it on Sunday and fire it all week, but the joke became less funny when we spent all day firing it.*

There were thousands of men in the prime of life who, this morning, thought they were destined to live to a ripe old age. I was standing next to several of them. One minute they're with me, the next they're on the ground, screaming in agony and terror.

Mostly there was nothing I could do. As soon as the men got hit, most were dead. But one of my best friends here, Lucius, got hit by a bullet in the leg. It tore a huge hole in his leg and shattered the bone into a million pieces. The bullet carried dirt, bits of his pants and, I can only assume, millions of germs into his wound. They told us in training we must get these wounds treated within 48 hours or infection would set in.

When Lucius was hit, it seemed to happen in slow motion. My feet were glued to the ground and I could only watch him as his faced filled with fear and pain, realizing he'd been hit. My first thought was, "I was standing there just a few seconds earlier. It could have been me."

I saw him looking at me, his eyes pleading with me to help him. I didn't know what to do. Should I continue fighting? Should I help Lucius? I knew if I left him and the Rebels took him prisoner, he would surely die. So I half carried, half dragged him to the field hospital, about two miles behind us. I got him back so the stretcher bearers could attend to him. I watched as they put him in a small gully that gave a little protection. It was very quiet back here in contrast to the deafening noise of battle we had come from. I heard a little moaning, but most everyone was quiet. The lucky ones had their canteens with them and could sip water while they waited for the surgeons to do what they could to help them.

I found an orderly and asked what would happen to Lucius. He told me they put the wounded in three categories: mortally wounded, slightly wounded and those needing surgery. He looked briefly at Lucius and told me his leg would be amputated. There were too many wounded to take much time with any one patient. If the wounds were bad, they'd just amputate to save time.

I looked around at the hospital. It was filthy. Everything was covered with dirt, blood and flies. The surgical instruments looked as if they hadn't even been wiped clean after the previous surgeries. It seemed hopeless that Lucius would come through this.

The orderly barked to the others, "This one can wait — he needs his leg off, though. Go take a look at those." He pointed to a new wave of wounded, some walking slowly, some carried on stretchers.

I realized I could do no more for Lucius and left him in God's hands. I gave him a small salute but could form no words of comfort.

As I made my way back to the front lines, I had to pick my way through the dead and dying. Some of them grabbed at my legs as I went passed. The first time it happened I was horrified, but in a few moments the shock of it deadened my sensibilities and I simply shook them off. If I could, I made them as comfortable as possible, handing them their canteens while I walked or shooing flies off their faces. But it was as if I were someone else, watching this spectacle through different, uncaring eyes. It wasn't that I didn't care. It was just too overwhelming. I couldn't do anything to help so my brain and emotions unhooked from the rest of me, allowing me to move through this valley of death.

The dead probably covered five acres of this battlefield. And I was walking through them as if I was back in the orchard, walking through it.

The closer I got to the front, the more chaotic it became. The air filled with sounds, quietly at first then reaching a deafening crescendo. I heard screaming from the wounded, commands shouted from the officers, swearing, praying and groaning. And the constant sharp blasts from the rifles. Because of the smoke, I could only see what was directly in front of me. I didn't know where the shots were coming from but I leaped into action and tore open my cartridges with my teeth to get powder in my gun. I saw some boys who were so scared and frantic, they would forget to take their ramrods out of their guns before firing, causing them to sail through the air.

We fought like this the rest of the day.

Then it was over.

The hiss of the shots died away and the voices quieted till all was silent. I was still alive! When I looked around, though, my tears fell freely. To think that we "civilized" men could kill one another like beasts was too much for me to bear.

Others were standing as I was, trying to understand, trying to wrap our brains around it all. Tearing open our cartridges with our teeth smeared black powder all over our faces. We looked like demons. I felt like a demon, too.

It was unfathomable that, in one short day, so many men died in so many horrible ways. And yet our officers were happy! They congratulated themselves and us on winning this battle. As if anyone but the devil "won" today.

But their enthusiasm was infectious and those of us left among the living, I am ashamed to say, rejoiced. We were simply happy we weren't dead. In spite of the horror around me, I felt proud that I did my duty, however unpleasant.

As I write this to you, I find myself reliving the day over and over again. The terror I feel doesn't stay with me constantly. In fact, I can readily go about the business of living, even joking and laughing on occasion. But then the terror comes back like a throbbing pain and I find myself standing in that bloody field all over again.

I can only hope our children and our children's children will never find themselves in this predicament. And I trust the Almighty hand that held me safe today will continue to guard me. I fear there is to be much more danger before me. If it is God's will that I find my grave on a battlefield, I hope to be ready. I will continue to serve honorably so you can be proud of me. I am determined to come home to you, but if I can't, please know that I love you all and think of you every minute of every day.

Your loving husband and father,
James

CHAPTER 43

Bringing in the Apples

Ruth was sitting around the kitchen table with her children all around. All had solemn faces, even little Emily, although she didn't quite understand the problem.

"Pa isn't likely to be walking through that door any time in the near future," stated Ruth calmly. "So, we need to bring in the apples by ourselves this year. Now Johnny has done a fine job tending the orchard —" she nodded at Johnny who beamed at the compliment — "but the hard part hasn't begun yet. We can't afford to hire a crew to help us pick the apples and we can't count on . . ." Ruth's voice trailed off and they all knew she meant they couldn't count on Sam's family to help. Neither Ruth nor Hanna had taken any initiative to get beyond the argument they had when the men went off to war.

She continued, "So we'll be doing it all ourselves. Your father is counting on us and I know we can do this."

Lydia said, very matter-of-factly, "Of course we can, Mother. When do we start?"

The pride she felt for her children overwhelmed Ruth.

At that moment, she was sure they could do it, too.

"We start tomorrow at first light. I don't know how long it will take, though. We'll just take each day as it comes. In the meantime, let's say extra prayers."

The next day promised to be clear and bright. It was a beautiful late October morning, with the sun just thinking about peeking over the hills in the distance. Ruth was ready to bribe the children out of bed but didn't need to as they all came laughing and talking down the stairs, ready for the day.

"Well, look at you! You're so bright and bushy-tailed, you probably don't even want any breakfast."

"Ma! Yes we do. We're starved. We've got a big day ahead!" protested Johnny, Lydia and Mary. Little Emily tugged on Ruth's apron. "My tummy is talking and it says it's hungry right now!"

Ruth laughed and scooped her up in her arms. "Emmy, you tell your tummy to get ready for the best breakfast it ever had. All of you, now, sit down and we'll eat," she instructed.

This *was* a feast! There was fresh milk, so cold it made condensation trickle down the outside of the stone pitcher. There were heaping bowls of porridge with huge bricks of butter melting in the middle. There were flapjacks as big as plates waiting for some of the locally tapped maple syrup to ooze down the sides with its sugary delights. There were three kinds of meat. They hadn't had any meat in awhile so this was surely a treat. There were thick slices of salty bacon, fried crisp like the children liked it. There were links of spicy sausages and slabs of sweet pink ham. And, finally, there were peaches floating in their delicious juice.

"Mary, will you say grace?"

"Dear Lord, thank you for all your blessings, and for all this good food. Help us do a good job today with the harvest. And make sure Johnny doesn't eat all the bacon before we get some."

Ruth tried not to smile but was unsuccessful. Everyone burst out laughing and began passing food and filling their plates. When they had all eaten their fill, the sun began shining through the kitchen window.

"We better get out there before it's time for lunch already," Ruth teased.

"Oh, don't say 'lunch' — I'm stuffed," groaned Johnny.

"Too much of that bacon, big brother?" teased Lydia, poking him in the belly, then running just out of his reach.

"I'll get *your* bacon, you little pest," laughed Johnny, chasing her around the kitchen.

Knowing she'd be sorry she left the kitchen a mess, Ruth also knew it would take too long to clean it up. She took one sad look around and wished some 'kitchen fairy' would wave a magic wand and clean it while they were outside. Oh, well, she sighed.

"Hey, save some of that energy for picking. Now let's go! March!" commanded Ruth.

The four children lined up behind her and began marching, pulling on sweaters as they went. One by one, the marching forced them to think of their father and they began walking side by side, silently.

Ruth noticed the change in her children. "Now, I reckon your father wants you to have fun while he's gone. He's at war — not you. I know you miss him and that's understandable, but there's no reason for you to be so solemn when you think of him. He'll be back in no time and when he comes home, he won't want you lookin' like you forgot how to smile. So let's work hard but have some fun too!"

With that, she started handing out assignments. "Mary, gather up all the bags. Then find all those bushel baskets and bring them out here. Put some at the top of each row so they're handy. Johnny and Lydia, help me with these ladders. Emmy, sit right there and wait for me. I have a very important job for you."

Emily climbed up on a tree stump and got busy inspecting some ants while she waited for her mother.

They had only been able to afford four tree ladders which were twenty two feet tall and very expensive. James had been planning to buy more with the profits from this harvest or at least try his hand at making some. His plan was to eventually have one for every tree because people can pick apples much faster when they don't have to move ladders around the orchard.

Johnny was at one end of the ladder, Lydia was in the middle, and Ruth was at the other end. Even with three people, the ladder was difficult to lean up against the tree, but they were finally successful. After they got the hang of it, they moved the remaining three ladders more easily.

When they finished, Mary stood still with the bags slung over her shoulder. "Give us each one, Mary, then lay the rest over there in case we need more," Ruth said.

The canvas picking bags had a strap so they could be slung crosswise over a shoulder to keep the pickers hands free. Mary slung one over her shoulder. "Uh, Ma?" she asked.

"Just a minute, let me think." Ruth was trying to puzzle out the most efficient way to move the ladders around the orchard so they wouldn't have to move any of them very far. "If we move that one over there, then that one to there . . ."

"Ma, I think I have a problem . . ." Mary started.

At the word 'problem' — especially on an important day like this — Ruth whirled around and gave Mary her full attention. "What is the . . . Oh!" Ruth began laughing at the sight of her not-entirely-big-enough six-year-old.

Mary had the canvas bag slung over her shoulder all right, but it went all the way down her side and was dragging on the ground.

"We can probably fix this," Ruth laughed. She grabbed up a handful of canvas at Mary's shoulder and deftly tied it into a knot.

Ruth used her best carnival barker's voice. "Okay, step right up for your own super-duper shoulder knot. Best one in the county. Everybody plays, everybody wins!"

"Okay, we're all ready. On your marks, get set, go. Get pickin'!" Ruth called after them, "And be careful. We've got no time for emergencies today!"

The children ran to the nearest trees. Mary ran to one without a ladder propped up against it. She stared at the trunk momentarily, then puzzled it out and ran to a tree with a ladder.

Ruth went over to where Emily was happily studying the ants. Ruth took her by the hand saying, "Here we go, Em. You ready to work?"

Emily nodded. She liked nothing better than to be helpful. It was just that a two-year-old's idea of helpful is often different from anyone else's.

Ruth led her out to the middle of the trees the children had already started picking. She squatted down, eye-level to Emily. "Can you point to a tree full of apples?"

When Emily did so, Ruth praised her. "Excellent! Here is your very important job. When we are up in the trees, in the middle of everything, we can't see which tree to pick next. You know the saying, *You can't see the forest for the trees?* Oh, well, of course you don't. You're two years old." Emily was looking so seriously at Ruth with her big blue eyes, Ruth just had to laugh. She started over. "We can't spend all our time looking around for the trees that need to be picked and moving the ladders all over the place. So your job is to tell us which trees still have apples on them. Can you do that? You'll need to talk loud and clear so we can hear you."

Emily nodded. "That tree, that tree, that tree," she began pointing all over the orchard.

Ruth laughed. "Excellent. But not until we ask. You sit here and play," Ruth drew a big circle in the dirt with her foot, "but don't get out of this circle unless I tell you to. We're counting on you, baby girl." Ruth turned and walked away. "We've *got* to make this work."

When Lydia saw her mother, she shouted, "Lookee, Ma! My bag's getting full!"

"Great! Keep working as fast as you can," Ruth called out. She knew that experienced adult apple pickers can pick 175 bushels of apples per day. After a little mental arithmetic, Ruth sighed a heavy sigh. "Ruthie, my dear," she said to herself, "this is going to be one long day."

"What, Ma?"

"Nothing, Johnny, just do your best."

Ruth climbed the fourth ladder, bunching her skirts up in one fist.

The orchard was quiet, just the sound of cicadas and crickets chirping in the sunshine. Occasionally, Ruth would hear snippets of songs Emily sang in her little baby voice. Each time it made Ruth smile. And each time she wished James was here to hear it, too.

They had been working hard most of the morning and had developed a rhythm and timing to their picking. Ruth, Johnny and Lydia were picking at about the same speed, so they would all climb down their ladders at about the same time, dump their load of apples into the bushel baskets, then move the ladders to new trees.

Johnny remembered Pa telling him about the apple crews. They'd call out, "Tree Man, show me a tree!" so Johnny began calling out to Emily when he had cleaned out the tree he was working on, "Tree-mily! Show me a tree!" Emily would giggle and point out a tree full of ripe apples. Now, they all called her Tree-mily. Ruth was resigned to the fact the nickname would stick.

The crew stopped for the picnic lunch Ruth had packed while she was making breakfast, then worked until dark when they went in for supper. They were all hot, tired and hungry.

Ruth took a look around the kitchen. None of the dirty dishes washed themselves since they left this morning, which seemed about a thousand years ago. Oh, well, Ruth sighed.

Emily had ants crawling all over her. Luckily, she thought of them as friends instead of insects and didn't seem to mind a bit.

Johnny laid down on the floor to pull his boots off and had fallen asleep right there on the floor. When Ruth saw him, she called to the girls to see him, but when they didn't answer her, she looked for them. They, too, had fallen asleep, heads together, leaning on each other in one of the kitchen chairs.

"Well, I guess that just leaves us, 'Tree-mily,' " said Ruth, tiredly.

Emily looked up at her. "We go night-night now?"

Before Ruth could answer, Emily was toddling off to her bed. Ruth knew she'd rather be sleeping than eating too, and followed her up the stairs. Halfway up the stairs she stopped, remembering the filthy kitchen.

"A mother's work is never done, is it?" She helped Emily get ready for bed, then went to clean the kitchen. After all, she thought, we just might want to eat breakfast tomorrow.

CHAPTER 44

We Are a Family

S ilas was sitting in the dirt, leaning against the fence watching the sheep in the pasture. He was worried. It was November already and it didn't look like his father would be back from the fighting in time for breeding season. He didn't want to worry his mother, but Silas didn't have any idea what his father did at breeding time. He was afraid to ask his mother because he didn't really think she knew either and then she'd be worried, too.

Silas just needed someone to talk to. He wished Johnny was around. Even if Johnny didn't know what to do, it always helped Silas clarify his own thinking when he talked things over with someone.

But Silas knew Johnny was still helping with the apple picking. In spite of himself, Silas couldn't keep away from the orchard and had spent an hour or so a few days earlier watching them pick apples. They seemed to be having fun doing it and Silas wished he could have found the courage to step out from his hiding place and help them. But he knew that even though he and Johnny had set aside their differences, their mothers hadn't. He wasn't sure of the reception he'd get from his aunt. He missed Ruth and cute little Em and Mary, and even that pesky Lydia. If it were only possible, Silas would change so many things.

Silas shook off his fantasy and tried to figure out what to do about breeding the sheep.

"Well, let's see. I'm a smart guy; I can figure this out. Hmmm . . . It makes sense that I should separate the ewes from the rams. And it makes sense that certain rams shouldn't breed with certain ewes — like their sisters. Now all I have to do is figure out how to tell the sheep what I think!" Silas giggled even though he was trying to be serious.

"Do you have an invisible friend or are you talking to yourself?" Silas hadn't heard his mother walk up behind him. She leaned on the fence post next to him and gently pulled a lock of his dark hair. "What's going on?"

"Aw, nothin' I reckon," he said unconvincingly.

"I reckon that's not entirely true," his mother said gently.

Silas was quiet a moment, then took a deep breath and spoke in a rush. "I don't think Pa is going to be home in time for breeding and I don't think I know what to do and I didn't want to worry you by asking."

Hanna was quiet for a long time. Finally, she said, "I see. So you were out here asking the sheep what to do instead of your mother who loves you very much and would always be happy to help if you had a problem."

Silas nodded while looking at the ground.

"Son, listen to me carefully. We are all in this together. If I had a problem, wouldn't you want to help me?" Again, Silas nodded. "So why don't you think I wouldn't want to help you? Besides, these are not *your* sheep; we are ALL responsible for them. We are a family and we work together. We take on each other's sorrows and joys. We help each other with problems and celebrate each others' accomplishments. Do you understand? We need to be here for each other. Especially if your father . . ." Hanna trailed off, not really wanting to go too far into their uncertain future.

"I came out here, Silas, because I need you to do something for me today. Remember the agreement we have with James and Ruth? They get the orchard started and we help them out until the trees produce? I have a couple of baskets of food to take over to them. But I . . . well . . . I'd rather not see them right now."

Silas looked at his mother with compassion. This was just as difficult for her as it was for him — maybe more.

"They're working in the orchard, Ma. We can just leave it on the porch."

Silas didn't want his mother to know he'd been spying at the orchard, but the look on her face told him she already knew. What he didn't know was how much she had wanted to go to the orchard, too.

They were both quiet for a moment, each thinking their thoughts.

"So, what did your invisible friend tell you to do about the sheep?" Hanna asked after awhile.

"Well, I think I need to separate the ewes from the rams and pick the rams carefully to get the ones with the best qualities. But I don't know how many ewes to put in with each ram. And where do I put the rest of them? I was thinking I could close off that area over there," he said, pointing, "to keep the rest of the ewes and the rams that aren't chosen. Then I'd put the breeders over there. And I reckon I need about thirty ewes for each ram."

"I think that sounds like an excellent plan. Well thought out, logical — yep, your pa would be proud."

Silas looked at his mother and smiled at her praise. He was glad to have someone to talk things over with, even if it wasn't Johnny.

As if she was reading his mind, she said, "It would be nice if Johnny, er, someone could come help us, though."

Silas just nodded slightly. "I'll start first thing tomorrow getting those fences built. Then we'll have lambs by April. Surely Pa will be home by then." Silas gave his mother a hug, then ran off to the barn.

Hanna watched him and sadly shook her head. "I don't think so, Sweetie. But I'll keep my fingers crossed."

CHAPTER 45

Bad News in Hadley

The apples were all in, the bushels had been sold and the kitchen was finally cleaned so Ruth and the children walked into town for some supplies.

Things were different in town these days. It wasn't anything they could put their finger on, but the atmosphere in town was quieter, less friendly, maybe a little sad.

Occasionally they heard about fighting in town when there weren't enough supplies. Once they heard that Mr. Owens and Mr. Gilford, both old-timers in the area, got into an actual fistfight because the blacksmith only had enough iron to forge one wheel rim but they both needed one. Luckily, the fight was soon over and more iron came into town the next week. But the bad blood remained.

Ruth and her children went up the steps to the general store for some flour and salt but learned that many of the supplies they needed were unavailable because of the war. Either they were going directly to the soldiers, or the factories were producing other things for the war.

Ruth understood, but that didn't make it any easier to do without. She couldn't remember when she had a real cup of coffee or sugar for baking. She kept her fingers crossed that Mr. Hawkins would have what they needed today. As they got to the door, they saw Mrs. Robertson.

"Well, hello, Agnes. How are you? Is everything going okay out at your place? Have you heard from your Max lately? We're hoping we have a letter from James waiting for us here," said Ruth.

"I'm fine, Ruth. I'm just trying to take things one day at a time."

As Agnes and Ruth gave each other a peck on the cheek, Agnes said, "But it is mighty hard, isn't it, being mama and papa and tending to all the chores. I'll be glad when my Max gets home. We haven't heard anything in a few weeks so we're hopin' — like you are — to get a letter today. How are you handling things out at your orchard?"

"We just got in all the apples, thanks to these hard working children of mine," she said proudly, smiling at little Emily resting in Ruth's arms. "John, here, has worked especially hard. His father would be very proud."

Johnny blushed so much, his face matched his hair; Lydia and Mary smiled shyly.

When Ruth and her friend Agnes began walking into the store, the children bolted ahead of them, hoping Mr. Hawkins was giving out free candy samples. The two women said their hellos to everyone inside, then asked if there was any mail.

"Well, I'm sorry, Ruth there isn't anything for you, but, Agnes, you did get something," Mr. Hawkins rummaged around in the Robertson's mail bin while Ruth went to weigh some flour. "Ah, here it is; it's official looking."

The color drained from Agnes' face as she opened the letter and read: "The Department of War regrets to inform you of the death of your husband, Maxwell C. Robertson . . ."

Agnes sank to her knees, wailing. Ruth ran to her side and Agnes clung to her, sobbing. They both sat on the floor sobbing while everyone else in the general store stood by, not knowing how to act. Slowly, everyone but Isaac Cleaver drifted out of the store, and eventually, Agnes quieted down.

Ruth said, "Johnny, pick up Agnes' packages and put them in Mr. Cleaver's wagon. Girls, wait for me outside on the steps."

Ruth helped Agnes to her feet then led her out to the wagon, saying gently, "Isaac will take you home. I'll fix my children their supper, then come out to your place later. You get some rest."

Johnny stood by his mother until the wagon was out of sight. Ruth heaved a big sigh, gathered her coat around her more tightly and said with no emotion, "James and Max Robertson were in the same camp. Remember that letter we got?" Then she picked up her flour and her salt and began walking home, the children following behind.

CHAPTER 46

Christmas Surprise, 1861

The Christmas season came around again in 1861, just like all the other years, but no one at either Jackman farm felt like celebrating. On December 23rd, Hanna finally got fed up with her children's moping around and decided to do something about it.

"Tomorrow morning there will be some changes around here," she announced. "First, we're going to find the most beautiful tree we can drag home. Then while we're decorating it, Silas will get us a wild turkey for Christmas dinner. And no one is going to be draggin' around here like it's the end of the world." Hanna softened a bit then continued. "I miss your pa, too, but he wouldn't want us to forget about Christmas. It sure won't be like it was last year when everyone came to visit, but . . ." she trailed off, knowing that the contrast between this year and last would be so overwhelming that even she didn't think it could be overlooked.

Hanna looked around at her three children. She attempted a smile that came out rather sickly and not at all happy looking. "Let's just try our best. . . . for your father," she ended lamely.

The children nodded weakly. As Silas and Elizabeth left the room, Abigail walked over to her mother and climbed up on her lap. Silently, she put her arms around Hanna's neck and snuggled her face into her mother's shoulder. Hanna was glad they couldn't see her tears.

After Hanna called the children in for their lunch, she began to put on her coat and scarf.

"Aren't you eating with us?" Elizabeth asked. "Where are you going?"

"I'll be back shortly," Hanna replied. "You two help Abigail and clean up the kitchen when you're done. I won't be long."

With that, she left the children to guess where she was going and what she needed to do.

After thinking a moment, Elizabeth said, "Oh! I know! She's going to get us our Christmas presents. Yippee!"

Silas said sharply, "Don't say that in front of Abigail. You know there's no money for gifts this year. What are you thinkin'?"

Elizabeth looked as if she'd been slapped in the face. She'd almost forgotten what the past year had been like.

Abigail began banging her spoon on the table and chanting, "Yippee! Yippee! Yippee!"

"Oh stop it!" Elizabeth turned on Abigail as Silas had turned on her.

"Both of you stop it!" Silas yelled.

The silence in the kitchen felt suffocating.

"I'm sorry. You're right. Maybe Ma did go to get us something for Christmas, but don't get your hopes up," Silas said gently. "Abbey, your spoon is not a toy."

They looked around at each other and began to giggle. "You sound just like Ma!" laughed Elizabeth.

This was how it was supposed to sound in their

house, filled with laughter and happiness.

"Let's finish up and surprise Ma by having everything done when she gets home . . . from wherever she went," suggested Silas.

"Now you sound just like Pa!" Elizabeth laughed even harder.

"Eat!" commanded Silas in his deepest, most Pa-like voice. The three of them convulsed into laughter and Silas felt as if he had helped all of them through a difficult time.

"Maybe this won't be such a bad Christmas after all," he thought to himself as he watched Elizabeth wipe the happy tears of laughter from her eyes.

When Hanna returned home, Silas noticed she looked very happy. Her cheeks were red and her eyes were bright and had a twinkle. Maybe she did buy us something. As quickly as he had the thought, he pushed it right out of his head. No reason to get my hopes up either, he thought.

"Children! Come here, I want to . . . hey! . . . Who cleaned up this house so well?"

Abigail ran to her mother and jumped up on her. "I pushed in all the chairs, and picked up all the food that fell off my plate, and Elizabeth even let me dry some of the plates."

Hanna wished everyone else was so enthusiastic about doing chores around the house. "That is so great, Sweetie!" Hanna walked around the table holding little Abbey. "I do believe these chairs have never been pushed in so well before. Are you sure the Cleaning Up Elf didn't help you?"

Abigail's eyes got as round as saucers. "No, Ma! I did it all by myself," Abbey bragged, then thoughtfully considered what her mother had said. "Are there really elves that help?" she asked.

"Well, I have three of them right here," and Hanna gathered them up in her arms and gave them all one big hug.

"Where did you go, Ma?" asked Elizabeth.

"Let me hang up my coat and I'll tell you," she replied.

The children knew it had to be something wonderful by the way their mother looked. Maybe she heard from Pa.

Hanna sat down and they clustered around her. "I went to see Ruth," she began. "They've been feeling as badly as we have, so we've decided to have Christmas together."

Abigail jumped up and down. "Yippee! Yippee! Yippee! Do I get to play with Emmy and Mary and Liddie again?"

"Yes! And Johnny, too! And your Aunt Ruth is desperate for an Abbey hug."

Silas and Elizabeth weren't quite sure this was good news. Silas said, "But what about all those awful things you both said. Aren't you mad at Ruth?"

Hanna chose her words carefully. "Ruth and I were — and still are — very scared and angry and unsure. But we are family. We had a long talk and realized all those things we had said are unimportant now. That was then; this is now. And now, I need Ruth and those kids. And they need us."

"But what changed? Pa and Uncle James are still gone and fighting against each other," interrupted Elizabeth.

"Yes, they are," agreed Hanna sadly. "But we're still here. And it's Christmastime and it's time to get over it," she finished brightly. But when she saw the puzzled looks on their faces, she asked, "Don't you want to have your cousins back?"

Silas and Elizabeth looked first at each other, then at their mother's worried face. They didn't want her to worry ever again and realized they did indeed want their cousins back.

They smiled at their mother. "This will be a great Christmas!" Elizabeth said as she flung her arms around her mother.

"Yes, it will," sighed Hanna and hugged Silas close, also.

Chapter 47

Hunting Christmas Dinner, Alone

Silas woke early the next morning, intent on bringing home another big turkey like they got last year. He remembered every detail of last year's hunting trip and could still hear the echoes of the charging bear's snarls as she came at them.

Gradually, he had fewer and fewer nightmares of that day. Instead, he began to remember the good parts as well. He remembered the pride he and Johnny felt when they successfully tracked the white-tailed deer and Johnny was able to kill it with his first shot.

He remembered the awe he felt after shooting his father's rifle. It's aim was so true, it was what they call a "sweet rifle." Silas realized that day it's true what they say — a bad gunsmith will never make a sweet rifle but a great gunsmith may only make one in his lifetime. This was one of those rifles and Silas intended to take excellent care of his father's gun until he returned.

And he remembered how funny it was seeing his Pa

and Uncle James showing them how to track wild turkeys. He smiled as he remembered Pa saying, "They are really dumb creatures, but you'd be surprised how stupid they can make you look." And was he ever right. The two men were trying to surround the turkey and herd it toward the clearing so the boys could get a clear shot at it. Unfortunately, just when they got close, the bird realized what was happening, gave a squawk and a jump, and ran back to where it felt safe again. The turkey was dumb enough, though, to continue this routine until he did, indeed, become a casualty.

It took a long time to shoot that turkey. But it was worth it. Silas could almost taste that turkey's tender drumstick again.

Then he quickly realized his reminiscing wasn't getting him any closer to another drumstick, so he set about getting the rifle loaded and got started.

There wasn't any snow on the ground like there was last year so Silas wasn't sure how he would be able to find any turkeys. He walked into the woods a little farther, then stopped to listen. He remembered the advice of his Uncle James that he and Johnny heard so many times: "Just look around the orchard. It will tell you what you need to do."

So Silas tried that. He looked around the woods and listened, expecting to know what to do. But he heard nothing.

He walked further into the woods and tried listening again.

Again, he heard nothing.

He was beginning to get discouraged and slightly nervous. What if he never found anything for Christmas dinner?

But he kept on.

Finally, after what seemed like days, he heard something off in the distance. He cupped his ear like he'd seen his father do a thousand times and just listened for a moment.

There it was again. He panicked momentarily remembering the bear. After all, he had heard the bear before he saw it, but this was different.

He walked very quietly toward the sound and soon he could identify it. Wild turkeys — and it sounded like lots of them!

Silas stood still, waiting to see which way they were coming from. He knew they'd never see him because they were busy foraging. He tried to remember if his father said they had good eyesight or poor eyesight. He was annoyed with himself that he didn't know. If he could remember, it might make this little escapade easier for him. He decided to err on the side of caution and assume they had good eyesight.

They appeared to be headed his way, more or less, so he just remained still. This was going to be easier than he thought. His gun was already loaded so, very slowly, he raised it to his shoulder. He held his breath, took aim and was just about to pull the trigger when his foot snapped a twig. Hearing the noise, all the turkeys simultaneously took off, running this direction and that.

Silas heaved a sigh, stood his gun in front of him and began to reload. At that moment, his emotions ranged from astonishment to anger to self-pity all at the same time, so it was understandable that he forgot he didn't quite get his shot off as he loaded a second charge.

The turkeys had all traveled a distance up ahead, but had quite forgotten the trouble they had just seen. They were quietly gobbling and looking for food once again. Silas followed them and came as close as he dared. He was getting cold and tired and really wanted to be on his way home so he was stepping extremely carefully. No twigs this time, he vowed.

When he had a clear shot at a beautifully plump tom turkey, he carefully raised the rifle to his shoulder, held his breath and pulled the trigger. For a split second nothing happened, then Silas realized he had made a terrible mistake.

The gun exploded out of his hand and flew several feet away. The turkeys leaped up and ran hysterically away from the noise. Silas felt searing pain rip through his hand.

Only then did he remember the words of warning from Uncle James: You must *always* know whether your gun is loaded or not. If you put another charge into your gun, it can burst and take off your fingers, your hand . . . or worse.

Afraid to look at his throbbing hand, Silas looked heavenward and offered up a silent prayer. *Please let my hand be there.*

He took a deep breath to calm down, then forced himself to look at his hand.

It was still there. Silas knew, though, that his injury was bad. The skin on the back of his hand and up to his wrist was burned and beginning to blister. The skin from the palm of his hand had blown off. His hand was bleeding heavily. He took off his jacket and shirt, then wrapped the shirt around his hand and tied the sleeves together to keep it tight. He struggled to get his coat back on, but his bandaged hand wouldn't allow that. So, he draped the coat over his shoulders and looked around for his father's rifle, afraid of what he'd find. It was worse than he thought. The gun had totally exploded. His father's beautiful sweet-shooting rifle, gone. Silas stared at it for the longest time before he bent to pick it up. As he was straightening up, something caught his eye.

He saw a turkey. It wasn't the beautifully plump tom turkey he was aiming for, but he had shot one after all. With a sigh, he picked up the scrawny bird and began the long walk home as it began to snow.

CHAPTER **48**

Christmas Argument

E lizabeth awoke to Abigail jumping on the bed.
"Lizzy! It's Christmas! And it's beautiful!" Abigail
pointed out the window.

Elizabeth humored her sister and pulled herself over
to the window to look outside. It *was* beautiful. The snow
glistened like diamonds wherever the sun danced over it. The
azure sky contrasted with the silvery white blanket of snow
laying over everything.

"Ooh!" squealed Elizabeth. The sight of it immediately put her in a holiday mood. "Let's go!"

They stopped in Silas's room and jumped on his bed.
"Silas! Wake up! It's Christmas!" shouted Elizabeth.

"And it's beautiful!" called out Abigail over her shoulder as she ran out of his room.

Silas turned over and pulled his quilts up over his
head.

He was still exhausted from his calamity-filled hunting trip to capture Christmas dinner the day before. And his

hand hurt like the dickens. His mother had cried when she saw him come home, but pulled herself together when Silas had begun sobbing in her arms. She cursed herself for letting him go hunting by himself.

His mother cleaned his hand for him, put ointment on the burn and bandaged it. Even though today was Christmas, they'd get the doctor out to take a look at it and make sure infection doesn't set in. So not only has Silas ruined his father's gun, his Christmas and his mother's Christmas, but he's also ruined the doctor's. This was not the happy holiday he had envisioned.

"Oh well, at least we'll have turkey for dinner," he consoled himself.

Silas dragged himself out of bed. As he dressed, he caught a glimpse of Abigail's beautiful day. For once she wasn't exaggerating. It was gorgeous! It was a day his father would marvel at and enjoy by sitting on the fence.

Silas stopped himself from becoming melancholy at the thought of his father on this very fine day. Wherever Pa is, he'll have a beautiful day, too — he won't miss it.

They all ate what their father would call a "stick-to-your-ribs" breakfast, then got busy preparing for their guests, at Silas' urging. However, if he knew just how bad the day would be for him, he wouldn't have been so excited.

Soon, he heard the door open and the sound of women and children laughing and talking. He ran down the stairs, then stopped a few feet from the bottom. He suddenly became nervous. As he quickly assessed his situation, he realized it was because he hadn't seen Johnny for so long. Would they still be friends?

As he stood around the corner on the stairs out of sight, his questions melted away when he heard Johnny ask excitedly, "Where's Silas?"

"Here I am," said Silas, a little shyly.

"C'mon!" Johnny said. "Let's go shoot marbles! Hey . . .

what happened to your hand?"

Silas began to tell him the whole story as they both ran to the barn, pulling on their coats on the way out the door.

"Oh! Hi, Aunt Ruth! Merry Christmas," called Silas over his shoulder.

Ruth and Hanna looked at each other with relief. "Looks like nothing's changed," said Hanna.

"Well, not *every*thing's changed, anyway," said Ruth.

Hanna nodded and they both watched the girls playing happily on the floor with their dolls.

"Let's have a cup of tea and talk," suggested Ruth.

Hanna told Ruth about Silas' accident and began catching up on other news. The boys were in the barn doing the same thing. Playing marbles was just a ploy to get off by themselves and talk.

"So, how is the orchard?" Silas asked.

Johnny began to tell him all about the harvest and how he was taking care of the trees when Silas interrupted him.

"I pretty much know all that. I . . . I . . . spied on you," Silas finally admitted.

"You what? You *spied* on us?!" Silas looked so sheepish that Johnny finally told him, "Yeah, me too. I saw you building that fence for the sheep. You were having so much trouble, I really wanted to help, but . . ." Johnny trailed off lamely.

"I know. I didn't know what to say, either, so I didn't say anything," Silas paused. "For too long."

"Good thing our mothers made up or who knows how long you'd have been so pigheaded!" Johnny laughed.

"What do you mean 'pigheaded'?" said Silas, annoyed.

Johnny explained, "Well, you must have known your pa was wrong to go off and fight for the South. It's like he's a traitor to his country. But you still never came over to apologize or anything."

Silas was furious. "Don't you ever call my pa a traitor. He is fighting an honorable fight, not like your pa. He's fighting so the states can govern themselves. Your pa is only fighting to free a bunch of slaves he's never even seen. How stupid is that?"

Johnny was stunned by Silas's outburst. After Johnny had processed the idea that they were already arguing again, he reacted to what Silas had just said. "Hey! My pa is not stupid. You take it back!"

"Won't."

"Will."

They took a step closer to each other, each threatening the other with their body language.

"Won't."

"Will!."

Fists clenched, another step closer.

"WON'T!"

"WILL!"

Their noses almost touched. They could see the hatred in each other's eyes. They stood that way for what seemed an eternity. Wisely, they each chose to back off.

Johnny walked away first. As he left the barn, he called over his shoulder, "Pigheaded! That's what you are!"

Silas was gathering up his marbles into his brown burlap bag. He narrowed his eyes and considered keeping Johnny's marbles. Instead, he scattered them all over the barn with his angry feet.

Ruth and Hanna were on their third cup of tea when they heard the door slam. "Maybe marbles wasn't the game to be playing if it makes them angry," analyzed Hanna.

The door slammed again and Johnny walked into the room. He glared at the two women sitting at the table. Then he backed up to the closest wall, crossed his arms angrily and slid down the wall until he was sitting on the floor. He propped his elbows on his knees, put his chin in his hands and stared at the floor.

Ruth raised her eyebrows at Hanna but neither said a word, even though they knew this was about much more than marbles.

Hanna stood up and motioned to Ruth with her head. They went into the kitchen to start making dinner. The boys needed to work this out themselves.

The girls played happily all afternoon. They played with their dolls; they played "Fox and Goose" outside by tramping down the snow into the game's round track; they made snow angels; they went inside and had a tea party; they played in the barn where they found what seemed to be a scavenger hunt for marbles. So they picked them up and played marbles for a while. When they tired of that, they picked each marble up one by one and pretended they were planets. The girls made up elaborate stories about who lived there and what they ate and what games they played. Then they tired of that, too. But there were so many games they hadn't played in so long, they had to make up for lost time.

While the girls were in the midst of a rollicking game of tag, their mothers called everyone in for dinner. Johnny and Silas dragged themselves to the table and made sure to sit at opposite ends. As the children sat down, it was difficult to hide their disappointment at the "feast" before them. It was nothing like last Christmas. There was only the scrawny turkey Silas shot, a big bowl of mashed potatoes, a loaf of bread and some green beans from the pantry. It seemed they never ran out of green beans.

Even though nothing was said, their mothers noticed.

When everyone was seated, Hanna said, "Who'll say grace?"

"I will," Ruth volunteered. "Dear Lord," she began while she collected her thoughts. "Thank you for this food. And I know I'd appreciate it if you'd help these children learn to be grateful. Even though they are disappointed we don't have any extras this year, help them to know we have more than enough food and they should be thanking you that their bellies are fixin' to be full."

She shot her own children a look they knew well. It was the "I-can't-believe-you're-acting-this-way-when-it-is-absolutely-not-the-way-I-raised-you" look. Then she continued.

"Thank you for helping us be together again. We all wish James and Samuel could be with us today, but that is obviously not your will. There are many hurts in our lives, Lord. Help us to deal with them and keep them in perspective. Amen."

Johnny wondered if he was the only one who knew his mother was actually delivering a lecture to them. He also wondered if that was okay with the Lord.

Dinner conversation was uninspired and contained many long pauses. The girls were tired from playing all day. The boys were not talking to each other, or anyone else for that matter. The children wanted more and different food. Hanna and Ruth tried their best to make this a festive occasion. But it was not to be.

Soon enough it was time for dessert. The children seemed to perk up a bit at the thought of dessert.

"Apple pie! Oh, no!"

"I'm sick of apples."

"Isn't there anything else?"

Ruth's children had certainly eaten their share of apples from the harvest, but she didn't realize they could be so spiteful about it. As she began to take their pie away, Johnny saw how hurt she was and said, "We're sorry, Ma. It's just that we thought today would be special and it's just . . . it's just . . . it just stinks!" Johnny glanced at Silas. "Your apple pie is great, Ma, but I don't think I want any tonight. Can I be excused?"

Ruth nodded and Johnny left the room.

"Does anyone want apple pie?" Ruth asked.

With one voice, Hanna and her children sang out, "We do!"

Ruth brightened when she realized some people had actually *missed* her apple pie. She gave them all big slabs of warm pie with the cinnamon juice running all around the plate.

When Emily, Mary and Lydia saw how much the others were enjoying Ruth's pie, they realized they were missing out.

"Can we have some, too?" they asked quietly.

"Of course you can . . . . as long as you quit complainin'!"

Hanna said, "When we're done, we'll clean up . . . then I have a surprise for you!"

With the promise of a treat, clean-up went quickly. They were finished in no time.

Hanna told them to wait in the other room with their eyes closed. When she instructed them to open their eyes, she was standing in front of them with brightly wrapped packages — one for each of them.

The girls each received a corn husk doll, each one posed differently. One was churning butter, one was gathering firewood twigs, one was picking flowers, one was holding a baby and one was carrying a bucket of water.

The two boys were both given a wooden top. Pulling the string made it spin and dance. The painted stripes created a feast for the eyes. Silas got a blue one and Johnny's was green.

"I traded Mr. Hawkins three of these corn husk dolls I made. I think he was going to give them to his daughters," said Hanna.

"That's great, Ma, thanks," said Silas unenthusiastically.

"Yeah, thanks, Aunt Hanna," said Johnny.

Any other time, the boys would be excited to have a

new toy. They'd usually rush outside and have some sort of contest right away. Today, though, Silas walked up to his room and Johnny went outside.

Hanna and Ruth watched them go.

"Open yours now," Hanna said brightly, trying to shake off the sadness she felt for the boys.

Hanna had given Ruth a handkerchief embroidered with pansies. "The hankie isn't new, but I bleached it and put your favorite flower on it."

"Oh, it's lovely! Thank you so much! With all the other work you've been doing, how did you find the time?" asked Ruth, putting an arm around Hanna's shoulder.

Hanna answered, "Well, sometimes I've been waking up in the middle of the night and I can't seem to get back to sleep. I hate to just sit there, so I keep my hands busy. It seems to help."

Ruth knew exactly what she meant. She walked over to where she put her coat and took out a small package. "I have trouble sleeping sometimes, too," she said as she handed it over to Hanna.

Hanna laughed as she opened a beautifully embroidered dress collar. They laughed and hugged. It was as good as Christmas could be expected to be for the Jackmans in 1861.

CHAPTER 49

Winter Picnic, 1862

Christmas crept away as silently and uneventfully as it came, leaving Hadley with a gray and limp January. The argument between Johnny and Silas seemed to hang heavy over the farm like a fog that wouldn't lift.

There were still chores to do in the orchard even though the trees stood sleeping. Late winter and early spring was the only time available to do many of the maintenance chores around the farm.

Lydia and Ruth were clearing the brush from under and around the apple trees. Mary was busy taking care that Emily stayed out of trouble, certainly not a seasonal job.

Johnny called to his mother, "Ma, have you seen that jar of nails I had out here yesterday?"

"No . . . have you tried looking in the barn?" his mother wanted to be helpful.

Of course he had tried the barn! What did she think he was — some stupid kid? Johnny decided against a smart-aleky response to his mother as it would only make her angry.

She was angry enough lately, he didn't need to help her in that department. In fact, she'd probably be able to scare away bears with the looks she gave lately.

"Oh, what a good idea, Mother," he sang out sweetly. "I'll try there next."

"Sheesh!" he thought to himself.

He walked into the barn half-heartedly looking for the nails, mostly looking for a place to sit and rest for a bit. As he sat on an old stump, a glimmer of light caught his eye. The jar of nails. Right where he'd left them yesterday.

"Oh, well, I can't be expected to remember *everything*," he mumbled grumpily.

He walked back out into the yard where the broken apple crates had been piled up. He swore the pile grew every time he looked at it. Johnny remembered the fun he and Silas had last year mending the crates. They had pretended that each swing of the hammer was the footstep of a giant stomping through their valley. Finally, they stopped him by tripping him with a huge rope, causing him to crash.

But that was a lifetime ago. Johnny was on his own this year.

"I'm never going to get all this done!" he complained. Quickly, he turned to see if his mother heard him. Luckily for Johnny, she had not. There was much work for all of them to do, with James still gone, and it made his mother mad as a wet hen to hear anyone complain.

Johnny got busy mending the apple crates. It was like a huge puzzle to work out. Broken boxes and individual slats were all jumbled up together. Some slats were too short for the sides he was working on, and some were too long. It reminded Johnny of the story his mother told him when he was small about Goldilocks and those three bears. One bed was too soft, one was too hard, and one was just right.

"If only I could find the 'just right' one for this crate," he mumbled.

As he attempted to solve the puzzle he had scattered all over the yard, he heard laughter and voices coming through the trees.

"Yoohoo! Anybody here?" Hanna's voice sang out from the trees. "We're tired of wooooorking — how 'bout yoooooooou?"

Johnny, Ruth and the girls stopped what they were doing with a laugh at Hanna's funny voice. Hanna, Silas, Elizabeth and Abigail burst through the trees carrying baskets.

"Picnic time!" shouted Elizabeth.

"How did you know we'd be out here starving?" laughed Johnny.

In unison, everyone finished the joke by saying, "Because you're always starvin'!"

Johnny and Silas eyed each other uneasily. Neither wanted to be the first to talk. When Lydia and the other girls began to open up the baskets and grab whatever tickled their fancy, Silas and Johnny decided silently to call a "picnic truce."

The war had created many shortages because much of the food grown was being sent to the troops, rather than sent to stores. Around Hadley, though, they rarely felt the tightening of their belts because they raised so much of their own food. They did miss the abundance of a few items they did not grow, however. Sugar and flour were rationed so the troops would have enough, but being talented cooks, Ruth and Hanna could make any shortages virtually unnoticeable.

Spices and other items from the South were impossible to get but nothing was really missed. The Jackman families simply used what was in abundance — the vegetables and fruits they had canned in the summer, the meat the boys were able to hunt, the items they could get from the general store when available.

In short, they made do with what they had and tried not to complain about what they didn't have. And they remembered how lucky they were they didn't live in a city where people couldn't have big gardens.

Ruth and Hanna watched the boys for a moment, then linked arms and went to sit on the blanket Hanna had brought.

"It's a little cold for a picnic, I know," said Hanna. "But it seems I've spent so much time being angry at the children lately, we all needed a break in the routine." She looked around at the half-cleared trees and the mound of broken apple crates in various stages of repair. "I hope you don't mind," she finished, alarmed they may have too much work to do to have a mid-day picnic. "I also thought it would be good for the boys. I hope I'm not pushing them."

"No, it's perfect, look at them," she gestured to the gaggle of children devouring food and laughing. "I think it's good for them to be together. Even if they don't make up." Ruth was quiet for a moment, then confessed, "I've been the same way with the children. When James left, he told me it would just be a little while until he came back. With every day that passes, I get more angry at him for not being here, which makes me feel guilty, which makes me more angry . . . . and it seems I take it out on the kids by being short with them. And I'm sick of apples. And it doesn't help that I'm exhausted all the time, either," she said wearily.

Ruth looked at the children. "They've actually been quite remarkable through this whole ordeal. I reckon they deserve some fun today. These crates can wait — they aren't going anywhere."

They watched the children for a few minutes, then

Hanna startled Ruth by shouting, "Hey! You're not fixin' to eat *all* that food are you?"

The children took the hint like squirrels take acorns — quickly and with gusto. They ran over to their mothers lugging the picnic baskets and each began offering the tempting morsels hidden inside.

"Alright, alright! Enough already! Give me a piece of that fried chicken and some of that cornbread," commanded Hanna. "Oh, and one of those apples." She looked apologetically at Ruth. "Sorry, but we don't eat apples nearly as often as you do!"

Ruth laughed and ordered, "I'll have a biscuit and a drumstick . . . but no apples for me!"

Johnny laughed at his mother and realized he hadn't heard her laugh for quite some time. It was good to hear her mirth and he told her so.

Ruth got quiet and Johnny was afraid he'd made her angry . . . again. But then Ruth said, "I haven't been fair to you children. I've been angry and tired and scared and . . . well, none of it's your fault. It's no one's fault and I've got to deal with it myself. You have your own problems."

Johnny and Silas had momentarily forgotten the argument they had. They glanced at each other to try and read what the other was thinking.

"You know," Hanna began, "it's perfectly fine to disagree with each other. Ruth and I have . . . well, let's say 'different ideas' about some things. But look at us. Best friends again."

"Yeah, but you were screamin' at each other," Silas reminded her.

Johnny piped up, "Some really mean stuff, too." Oops, had he gone too far? He held his breath and closed his eyes, saying a silent prayer.

Ruth looked at him with his face all scrunched up and laughed. "Yes, I reckon we did indeed say some ugly things to each other. We were mad," she shrugged her shoulders and looked at Hanna. "I think we probably still believe the same beliefs, deep down, but the anger is gone so we can think more clearly. I think I probably understand what Hanna is thinking about this war and she probably understands me now, too."

Hanna nodded. "Because we've had a chance to think about it, and," she added, "our lives now are different than they were on that day. Much has changed since then. Not only does that allow for clearer thinking, but it gives us something called 'empathy.' Have you ever heard that word?"

The children all shook their heads.

"Empathy is when you can put yourself in someone else's shoes. Lydia, remember yesterday when Mary wanted your doll? You gave it to her because you knew I was washing hers. You put yourself in her shoes and knew how you'd feel if you were Mary. Or when we can all feel the pain Silas must be feeling in his hand."

Everyone looked at the bandage, now a bit smaller, but still there.

"We do it all the time, mostly without even thinking about it," Ruth said.

"But sometimes it's hard, and sometimes you must think about it, right, boys?" prodded Hanna.

Silas and Johnny looked shyly at their mothers. How did mothers get to be so smart?

They looked at each other. Johnny said, "Well, I reckon this is the end of the lecture. They must want us to do something now."

Silas took his cue from Johnny and teased, "Yes, but what? I can't for the life of me figure out what to do. What *were* they talking about?"

Elizabeth looked at them curiously and cocked one eyebrow. "They want you to be friends again," she said seriously.

Everyone laughed at her earnestness.

"Yeah, alright," said Johnny, getting up.

Silas mussed Elizabeth's hair and said, "If you say so, Lizzie."

The boys each grabbed another biscuit and headed off toward the barn. As they ran off, they heard Johnny ask Silas, "Hey! Have you seen my marbles around?"

Ruth looked at Hanna and held up her crossed fingers. "Here's hopin'!"

Hanna nodded, held up her crossed fingers and said, "Here's hopin' for a lot of things."

CHAPTER **50**

Letter From Sam

Confederate Camp
Somewhere in Tennessee
December 28, 1861

My dearest Hanna, Silas, Elizabeth, and Abbey,
*We've been on the move so much lately that I haven't
had a chance to write. I don't even have much time to write
now as we'll be moving again shortly. I did want to send a note
to let you know all is well with me, however.*
I trust you are all taking care of one another.
*Christmas was dreadful and nothing has gotten better
since. We've had hardly any food, lots of rain and I think I am
catching some kind of illness. I expect it isn't too serious,
though.*
*I just heard the command we are to move out. We are
in a hurry to meet up with more Virginia Volunteers but they*

rarely tell us where or why. I'm a good soldier, though, I do what I'm told. Will write more when we settle into our next camp.

Until then, remember I love you all and pray for our homecoming — soon!

Your loving husband and father,

Sam

CHAPTER **51**

I Want My Grandkids To Enjoy These Trees

The wet weather of April finally gave way to the milder weather of May, allowing Johnny to plant the new crop of seedlings for the orchard at last.

He stopped digging long enough to wipe the sweat from his face with a soggy red bandana. He had grown taller and stronger in the past year. His father wouldn't recognize him if he walked up the path right now. But Johnny knew that was unlikely to happen.

As he rested, leaning on his shovel, he remembered last year — was it only last year? — when his father showed him how to plant the seedlings. He remembered how scared he was that he'd do the wrong thing: not dig the holes deep enough or snip off too much of the roots. Then he laughed out loud at the thought of the flop sweat that flowed when Pa said he could trim the trees.

After a year of doing all the work, now trimming was just another thing to be done. He had more holes to dig, then he had to unwrap all the seedlings, trim them and plant them. He wanted to finish early and go fishin', but it didn't look like that would be happenin' today.

He turned back to his digging. After a few minutes, he felt funny, as if someone was watching him. As he listened, he heard a twig snap and whirled around. His mother, his aunt, his sisters and his cousins were all standing there, watching him.

"What the . . . ! You scared the life right outta . . ." He stopped when he saw the tear-stained cheeks of his family.

Silently his mother handed him an envelope. He saw it was from the Department of War. A wave of fear washed over him. He opened the letter and began to read.

April 28, 1862

Dear Mrs. Jackman,

I am a chaplain in the Union Army. I regret to inform you that your husband, James Jackman, died soon after the Battle at Shiloh, Tennessee, which raged April 6th and 7th.

While I am saddened by this heavy burden of information I must give you, I have more news for you and your family in which you may find some comfort.

As you know, Samuel Jackman, James' brother, was also fighting in this war, but for the South. The Battle at Shiloh was very big; many men were involved on both sides. By coincidence, both James and his brother Sam found themselves on the battle-field at Shiloh.

James was fighting a different enemy, however, that of disease. Your husband was suffering from pneumonia, which is what killed him. All the months of sleeping on the wet ground and in damp, cold weather made him susceptible to infection.

Sam was taken prisoner during the battle because he, too, was in a weakened state. He was undernourished and had contracted smallpox.

There was nothing to do for either of them except pray with them and make them comfortable.

They did not know the other was in the same field hospital, but as I was making my rounds and talking with the different soldiers, I heard the same name. When I asked James if he had a brother named Sam he said, "I do, indeed, Chaplain. But I fear he will never know how sorry I am for the way we left things when we went off to fight. Could you help me write to him?"

I told him I could make a 'special delivery' and had two men carry Sam to James.

They had two days in which to reminisce and make their amends before Sam died. James died a few days after. I heard them laughing and talking about all sorts of memories and I know they had left behind very happy lives. They both knew they were dying and had tried to comfort themselves and each other with their happy memories.

Both men asked when I wrote to you to make sure you all knew how much they loved and missed all of you. They also wanted you to know how sorry they were to leave you like this, with all the work on the farms.

The money enclosed is all they had. They wanted you to have it.

Samuel's wife should be expecting official word of her husband's death, but as a man of God, I felt it was my duty to inform you of what I had witnessed.

I pray for your husbands' souls and for all of you in your time of sorrow.

I remain,
George Witherspoon
Chaplain

Johnny folded up the letter and returned it to its envelope. Then he hugged his mother and said nothing.

Hanna touched Silas' cheek gently with the back of

her hand. "You must always remember what these men did. They sacrificed everything for what they believed in. They were trying to make things better for you. They were honorable men."

Ruth, choking back her tears, said, "Yes, they were great men and we'll all miss them. But maybe the lesson we should learn is to understand and appreciate differences in people and in their opinions. It's a fine line to fight for what you believe in, but there must also be a place in your heart for compromise and compassion."

Ruth and Hanna helped each other to the house, holding Abigail and Emily's hands. Silas sniffled and blew his nose, then picked up the shovel and began to dig a hole. Elizabeth, Mary and Lydia, crying softly, began unwrapping the burlap from the sapling's roots and removing the moss.

Johnny picked up the clippers in one hand and a sapling in the other hand.

"Before we plant these, we have to trim off the unhealthy roots and trim the branches so they're uniform. But the most important part is to plant them exactly right."

Silas leaned on his shovel and added, "And never put off till tomorrow what needs to be done today."

Johnny stopped and wiped away a tear with his sleeve. "Besides, I want my grandkids to enjoy these trees."

What Do YOU Think?

• What do you think were the most important causes of the Civil War?

• What do you think about Abraham Lincoln's decision to send food in unarmed ships to Ft. Sumter?

• What do you think would happen today if a state wanted to secede?

• What do you think your life would be like if you were a slave during the time of the Civil War?

• What do you think you would have done with the ending of this story? Write it!

• What do you think of the practice of men hiring substitutes to go fight in their place during the Civil War?

• What do you think about John Brown's actions in Harpers Ferry?

• What do you think you would miss most about your life now if you were magically transported back to live on a farm in 1860?

• What do you think would be better in 1860 than it is now?

I'd love to see your answers to any of these questions, if you'd care to share them. Send them to me at Ampersand Press — the address is in the front of the book. Thanks!

For Further Reading

Civil War
- The Civil War in the American West
  by Alvin M. Josephy

- Between Two Flags
  by Lee Roddy

Slavery
- Fighters Against American Slavery
  by Stephen R. Lilley

- Bound for America
  by James Haskins

Abraham Lincoln
- Abraham Lincoln: President of a Divided Country
  by Carol Greene

- If You Grew Up With Abraham Lincoln
  by Ann McGovern

Cowboys
- Reflections of a Black Cowboy
  by Robert H. Miller

- Trail Fever: The Life of a Texas Cowboy
  by DJ Lightfoot

There are gazillions of fascinating books on every subject imaginable at your local public library. If you can't find these, use your library's catalog system to find topics of interest to you. If you don't know how, have the librarian show you. People who know how to use the library lead fuller, more interesting lives.

"This book would make a great gift!"

Share the joy of reading with someone you love.

Check with your local bookstore or order here.

YES! I want _____ copies of *An UnCivil War — the Boys Who Were Left Behind* at $9.99 each, plus $2 shipping per book. Colorado residents, please add 47¢ sales tax per book. My check for $ _____ is enclosed.

Please allow 15 days for delivery.

YES! Add me to your mailing list. I want to be notified when the next book in this series is available.

Name

Address

City/State/Zip

Email   Fax

YES! I want my **FREE GUIDE** *"Reading Maniac — Fun Ways to Encourage Reading Success"* (a $5.95 value). Send your self addressed, stamped envelope to:

Free Reading Maniac Guide

Ampersand Press

POB 3827

Parker, CO 80134

We'd love to hear any questions or comments.
Write to us or email us at AmpersandPress@aol.com

"This book would make a great gift!"

Share the joy of reading with someone you love.

Check with your local bookstore or order here.

YES! I want _____ copies of *An UnCivil War — the Boys Who Were Left Behind* at $9.99 each, plus $2 shipping per book. Colorado residents, please add 47¢ sales tax per book.

My check for $ _____ is enclosed.

Please allow 15 days for delivery.

YES! Add me to your mailing list. I want to be notified when the next book in this series is available.

Name

Address

City/State/Zip

Email   Fax

YES! I want my **FREE GUIDE** *"Reading Maniac — Fun Ways to Encourage Reading Success"* (a $5.95 value).

Send your self addressed, stamped envelope to:

Free Reading Maniac Guide

Ampersand Press

POB 3827

Parker, CO 80134

We'd love to hear any questions or comments.
Write to us or email us at AmpersandPress@aol.com